Melvin Grigsby

The Smoked Yank

Melvin Grigsby

The Smoked Yank

ISBN/EAN: 9783337343934

Printed in Europe, USA, Canada, Australia, Japan

Cover: Foto ©Andreas Hilbeck / pixelio.de

More available books at **www.hansebooks.com**

SMOKED YANK,

BY

MELVIN GRIGSBY.

SECOND EDITION.   ILLUSTRATED

CHICAGO:
REGAN PRINTING COMPANY.

1891

Dedication.

To the Real Chivalry of the South,

the old "Aunties" and "Uncles" and Valorous Young Men,

who so generously and bravely,

at the risk of Cruel Punishment and sometimes of Life,

Fed and Warmed and Hid and Guided

Escaped Union Prisoners,

As a Token of Gratitude this Little Volume

is Tenderly Dedicated

By the Author.

PUBLISHER'S NOTICE.

Not long ago the publisher of this book and several others met in the office of Mr. Grigsby. The subject of our conversation was the reviving interest in war stories and reminiscences, evidenced by the prominence given to that class of literature by all the leading magazines of the day. Incidentally, Mr. Grigsby remarked that he had, in manuscript, a book written several years ago, narrating, what his sons called, his "Adventures in the War," which he designed, sometime, to have published in pamphlet form for distribution among his relatives and friends.

Having previously heard that his experiences as a soldier were of an unusually varied and interesting character, my curiosity was aroused, and, yielding to my solicitations, Mr. Grigsby finally permitted me to see his manuscript. A careful reading convinced me that were it published in book form it would meet with a favorable reception, not only by the relatives and personal friends of the author, but also by thousands of veterans and sons of veterans, by all, in fact, who take an interest in the stirring incidents of our civil war.

Frankly believing this, I persuaded Mr. Grigsby to have the book published under the title of the "Smoked Yank," and agreed to be responsible for the success of the enterprise. Whether or not my judgment was well-founded is for the public to determine.

To my request for a preface, the author replied: "You have assumed the responsibility, and if you deem that explanations or apologies are due the reader, make them yourself." The publisher has none to offer.

SAM T. CLOVER.

PREFACE TO SECOND EDITION

The real preface to this book is contained in the first chapter. This Second Edition, with Illustrations, goes out because the first was received with favor by the public, and the Author is daily in receipt of orders which he cannot fill.

THE AUTHOR.

CONTENTS.

ILLUSTRATIONS.

Kit and Betty, old friends of my boyhood.

Escape of General Pillow.

A slave-owner in a bad fix.

The charge of a runaway horse.

"What in hell are you pointing your gun at this Yank for? He is my
  prisoner."

The captain of the "Sea Horse Cavalry" loses his boots.

We enter Andersonville.

Shot at the dead line.

Dead Yankees become articles of merchandise.

"If you 'uns thought dah' was Yanks in dis wagon I could jus' dance
  juba on you 'uns coat tails."

Captured by a fourteen-year-old boy.

Bloodhounds in sight.

"Eager for a glimpse of the damsel."

"Say, dah, young massa ! Can you paddle a canoe?"

Guided through a swamp by runaway slaves.

"There, with colors flying and band playing, go the boys in blue."

KIT AND BILLY, OLD FRIENDS OF MY BOY-HOOD.

THE SMOKED YANK.

CHAPTER I.

TELLS HOW THIS BOOK CAME TO BE WRITTEN.

For nearly twenty years I have been about to write this book. I came home from the war in 1865, a boy of only twenty years, but with a discharge that showed almost four years' service in the army. How vividly I recall this scene—getting off the stage at my native village I started to my country home on foot. Ascending a hill, I saw over the top a team coming towards me, Kit and Betty, old friends of my boyhood. My first rides were on their backs. But who is driving? Can it be father? He looks too old to be father. I stopped in the road. The bowed head was raised. Who could paint the changes that came over his face as he came toward me? He has told me since that he was thinking of me and wondering if he would ever hear of me again, when, raising his head to try and drive away his sorrowful thoughts, he saw me standing in the road. His lost boy. More than a year of anxious watching and waiting since those lines had been received saying, "Your son has been taken prisoner," and in all that time not another word, and then when trying to resolve to give me up, to raise his eyes and see me standing in the road, it was indeed a surprise.

My sons, never keep back glad tidings from anxious parents to give them a greater surprise. I ought to have sent them word of my safety at the earliest possible moment after reaching the Union lines. That was twenty years ago, and your grandfather looks as young to-day as he did then—he had been worrying. Coming home from the war an escaped prisoner—supposed to have died in Andersonville, I told my story very willingly to willing ears for awhile, and then it got to be tedious, even to me.

For several weeks I was the hero of that neighborhood. Visitors thronged my father's house to see the escaped prisoner and to hear of Andersonville and other rebel prison pens, and of my escape. To each new party, I told the story until to me it grew old and stale, and, to avoid continuous repetition, I declared my intention of writing it up for publication. When I tried to do so, I found that to hold a little audience of friends and relatives in seeming rapt attention, was vastly easier than to write a connected and readable narrative of the same incidents. I often began, but never advanced to the end of a satisfactory beginning, and finally postponed the work until I should acquire through reading and education a better command of language.

Thus I became a veritable procrastinator—though continually postponed, the purpose of writing my experiences in the war and publishing the narrative in book form was always present—I was always about to begin. To new friends and acquaintances of my school life, I would occasionally relate some incident of prison

life or escape and seldom found unwilling ears to listen,
or lack of encouragement when I mentioned my intention of writing a book. Whether they were, many of
them, bored by my monopolizing the conversation and
making myself the big ego, and thought the readiest
way to escape further infliction was to advise and
encourage the book plan, has often since been a
question in my mind, especially when I have realized
how easily I find it to be thoroughly bored in a
similar way.

Nevertheless, that self-appointed task was never
more than postponed. It has continued to be both my
waking dream and the cause of much self-condemna-
tion for not having performed the work earlier.

At first the fancied distinction to be acquired was
probably my strongest inducement to write. Later
the idea of great gain by means of such a book was not
absent. But now as I begin, I trust for the last time, to
carry out the long-cherished and often abandonded
scheme, neither the desire for notoriety nor the hope of
gain, is the moving cause.

Other hopes and dreams and plans of those twenty
years that have gone have not been fruitless—my home
is not now my father's house—there has been a cradle
in my own, babies on my knee, and, now two boys, one
nine and one ten, with the life of Alexander, of Hanni-
bal, and of Cæsar fresh in mind, are ever teasing me
to tell them of my life as a soldier.

"Papa, did you have any adventures when you
were in the war?" says Sioux. "O, yes, I had a good
many, such as they were." "Tell them to us," says

George, "we would rather hear about yours than read those in the books." And when I tell them some and then speak of time for bed, I know from the look of keen interest in their bright eyes, and the reluctance with which they go, that they have not been bored. And I tell them I will begin at once and write my adventures, as they call them, all out, and have a little book printed for them to read.

" Oh, won't that be jolly," says George, "to have a book all about Papa." "And I guess mamma and grandpa, too, and lots of other folks will want to read it," says Sioux.

They go to bed and I begin. If I do not finish before these boys are too old or too wise to care for so plain a tale in such crude fashion told, then perhaps boys of theirs may come and prize the book grand-father wrote, and perhaps some old soldier, worn with toil and weary of the present days, may let it lead him back to the old camp ground or prison pen, and thus beguile a pleasant hour.

CHAPTER II.

As it is easier to describe the actions of men than
it is to set forth the thoughts, feelings and motives that
moved them to action, so I expect to find much less
difficulty in narrating all that I did or saw, worthy of
mention while a soldier, than in telling why I became one.

I had not passed my sixteenth birthday when the
war began. I was a farmer's boy. Had been brought
up on a farm near the village of Potosi, in Grant county,
Wisconsin. A few winters at school in the old log
school house of our district and two or three terms at
the school in the village, had been my opportunities for
education. You, boys, have already read more books
than I had at that time. Such books for boys as
Abbott's Series of Histories had not then been written,
and probably would not have found their way to many
log farm houses if they had been. But I had read the
History of the American Revolution, had spoken at
school the famous speech of Patrick Henry, and I
loved the soul-stirring strains of the Star Spangled
Banner. My grandfather was a soldier of the war of
1812. His grandfather, who was known as " Revolu-
tionary John," fought in the war of the Revolution.
Many of the leading incidents of the history of the
country, especially of the wars and of the early settle-

ments in Virginia and Kentucky had been handed down from father to son in stories and traditions, and to these I have always been an eager listener.

I was well posted too, on the political questions that had for a long time agitated the country, for I had been a constant reader of Horace Greeley's New York Weekly Tribune. I can remember well the drubbings I used to get at the village school when the boys divided for snow-balling, into Fremonters and Buchananites. The Fremonters, to which I belonged, were largely in the minority. I can remember, too, the woes of "bleeding Kansas," and how I used to urge my father to take me with him out to Kansas so that we might help to put down the "border ruffians" from Missouri.

The firing on Fort Sumpter was quickly followed by Lincoln's proclamation calling for seventy-five thousand volunteers. These were to serve for three months. A company was at once formed at Potosi. I wanted to go. The men who had so long been threatening to dissolve the Union because they could not have political matters their own way, had at last fired upon the national flag, upon the Stars and Stripes.

As I saw in imagination the bombardment of Fort Sumpter, and the hauling down of the dear old flag, it seemed to me that I could see too, the landing of the Pilgrim Fathers, the "starving time" of the Jamestown settlement, the Indian massacres: the battles of Lexington and Bunker Hill and Brandywine; Washington crossing the Delaware; the awful winter at Valley Forge; the heroic deeds of Marion, and Sumpter, and

Jasper, and Newton; the glorious victories of our navy
in the War of 1812; every scene of hardship and of
heroism that had helped to win for us and to preserve
for us our proud position among the nations of the
earth, of which that dear old flag was the emblem, came
trooping up in memory. "The mystic chords of memory, stretching from every battlefield and patriot grave"
had indeed been "touched" but not "by the better
angels of our nature."

Such were the thoughts and feelings that impelled
me with an almost irresistible impulse to volunteer as a
soldier and help to chastise the traitors who had insulted the flag. Such, at least, are the thoughts and feelings that I would have described had I then attempted
to explain why I wanted to be a soldier.

There was another reason which I would not have
given then, and I cannot even now without a blush ; I
was desperately in love. If there was any doubt about
my desire to do battle for my country from purely patriotic motives, there was certainly none about my
readiness to go to the wars, or to engage in any other
affair of the knight-errantry order that might win smiles
of approval from the girl I loved.

But I could not go. I was the second in a family of
eight children, all girls. except myself and the youngest.
My father had gone to Pike's Peak, in the spring of 1860.
In the fall of that year he had started to cross the
mountains and we had not since heard from him—I
could not leave my mother with the management of the
farm and the support of the family on her hands. I saw
that company formed in line, dressed in their stylish

new uniforms of gray, heard the farewell speeches, saw flags and swords presented, saw them receive the warmest of kisses from all the lovely maidens for good-bye, and I turned away with a heavy heart, with tears of sore regret, and went back to my dull farm-work.

That was my last summer's work on a farm, and I have always been proud of the record I made. Besides putting in and tending the crops on all the ploughed land, I had twelve acres of land, on which there was a heavy growth of saplings and underbrush, grubbed and broken. We raised an excellent crop.

I did not neglect the farm, although my heart was not in the work. No boy of adventurous disposition who has an inherited love for dog, and horse, and gun, will ever be content on a farm while there is war in his own country. I had owned a dog and gun, and had been a hunter from the time I was eight years old, and I could ride like an Arab. My leisure hours during that spring and summer were devoted to such exercise as I thought would best fit me for the cavalry service. I took lessons in sword exercise from a man in the village, kept a young horse for my exclusive use and practiced him jumping over fences and ditches, riding down steep hills at full gallop, and shooting from his back.

The harvesting was all done and the grain ready for stacking when father got home. He had been snowed up all winter in the mountains of Colorado. My first thought was, now I can go to the war. My cousin, James F. Ayars, had enlisted in the 7th Wis. Infantry, and I tried hard to persuade my father to let me go in the same company. He thought I was too young —said that if I went into the army and survived the war, my opportunity for securing an education would be gone. He did not believe a boy would retain a desire for education through years of soldier life. He offered to send me away to school, and as the academy to which he proposed sending me was at Lancaster, the county seat, where the object of my boyish affections was then living, I concluded to follow his advice, and accept his offer.

Early in September I was duly installed as one of the pupils at the Academy, but I could not shake of the desire to take part in the war. In the latter part of November, C. C. Washburn, afterward General, came to Lancaster and made arrangements to have a company of cavalry recruited in that county. I went at once to the recruiting office. Was told that I would not be taken without the written consent of my father. How was this to be obtained ? I sat in school that afternoon with a book open before me thinking over the situation. Classes to which I belonged were called, but I was so deeply engaged in meditation that I took no heed. All at once the thought came to my mind that thousands of the young men who were at the front had left schools and offices and clerkships and, by serving their country, were losing opportunities for education and for professional and business advancement—that the country would have but few defenders if only those who could do so without sacrifice were to volunteer— these thoughts flashed into my mind, as sunshine some-times flashes through a rift in the clouds, and seemed to make the path of duty plain. I gathered up my books and without so much as by your leave, to the professor or any one else, I walked out of the school-room.

In the twinkling of an eye an obedient son, who never before had dreamed of wilfully disobeying his father's command, had been transformed into an un-compromising rebel.

Out of doors a cold sleeting rain was falling, and the wind blowing, but what would a soldier amount to who cared for a driving wind with sleet and rain? To procure a horse and gallop him over the twelve miles to my father's house was but an hour of sport.

The family were at supper when I entered dripping with water and splashed with mud. "Why, what in the world?" said mother. "What brought you home through such a storm?" "Soldiers don't care for storms, mother," I replied, and as I spoke my father looked into my eyes. He saw that I had crossed the rubicon.

That night we talked it over. I told him that I had resolved to be a soldier, and that if he did not give his consent, so that I could go in the company for our own county, it would only cause me to find some other place where I could enlist without any consent. He gave his consent but with great reluctance.

Boys, I was wrong, but I did not then think so—no argument or persuasion could at that time have created a doubt in my mind. "Honor thy father and thy mother and thy days shall be long in the land which the Lord thy God giveth thee," has a different meaning to me now. I can see now that if I had remained at school in obedience to my parents' wishes, although they might have erred in requiring me so to do, the responsibility would have been theirs, not mine.

"But what became of the girl?" says one of my boys after listening to this point. So that's the way the wind blows already is it? You would rather have a love story than a war story would you?

Well, boys, there isn't much to tell in the love story line. I shouldn't have mentioned the little there is were it not to let you see how nearly related love of country, which we call patriotism, is to all the other noble passions. No boy can truly love a chaste and modest maiden without having all the better qualities of his nature quickened and developed. He no sooner feels the tender passion than he wants to look better and do better, and be better. The fires of ambition are usually kindled by love of woman. One of the most refined and intellectual mothers that I ever knew used often to say that she never had any anxiety whatever about her boys when they were in love. She said there was no danger then of their forming any loaferish or ungentlemanly habits.

If she was right, and I believe she was, I had little opportunity for bad habits when I was a boy, for I was almost always in love. My affection for Helen began when we were but children; I was but thirteen and she a half year older in years, but many years older in manners and in the knowledge of social etiquette. I was an awkward country jake, she a village belle, admired by all the village beaux. It was not her handsome face nor her graceful, slender form, nor her bright and

laughing eyes that took my fancy, but all of these com-
bined with a daring and venturous disposition. I taught
her to ride on horseback, to fish, and to shoot, these were
the sports that we both loved best.   We ran races,
swam our horses across rivers, shot wild pigeons, and
even stole apples and water melons out of pure devilment, for we had an abundance of them at home. Yet
I never went to see her openly or avowedly as a lover.
I was too bashful, too green, perhaps, for that.

She and my oldest sister were chums, and I tried
hard to chum with her youngest brother. I used often
to walk two miles to town after a hard day's work for
no other purpose than to meet her, if possible, by chance.
Have often hid behind a bunch of lilac bushes and
thrown gravel stones at her chamber window, striving
thus to catch even a glimpse of her face. If you should
ever visit your grandfather's old homestead, go down
into the pasture, and there, beside an old road you will
see an oak tree with twenty-one scars, one above the
other. Each of them represents a blow of my axe and
a word of a vow made to Helen.

These are pleasant memories. Your Aunt Alice
could perhaps tell you more. After I had enlisted and
just before my company started for the war, she arranged
that never-to-be-forgotten visit that I made to the dear
old home with "another not a sister." Ask your aunt
to show you two pictures that she has in one case. One
of your father taken when he was sixteen, the other,
taken on the same day, of " the girl I left behind me."

CHAPTER III.

CAMP WASHBURN—I GET MY NAME IN PRINT—PRIVATES
EAT SANDWICHES IN THE RAIN, WHILE OFFICERS HAVE
CHAMPAGNE UNDER SHELTER—BENTON BARRACKS—ON
THE MARCH—I MAKE A RASH PROMISE.

At the time I enlisted, the company was quartered
at Patch Grove, in Grant county. There we were
drilled until about January 1st, 1862, when we joined the
remainder of the regiment at Camp Washburn, in
Milwaukee.

That was a hard, cold winter, often referred to as
the winter of the deep snow. The barracks were large
board shanties, filled with two-story bunks for the men
to sleep on; there was an adjoining room to eat in.
These shanties were so open that a laconic English boy
was not far wrong when he said: "The crocks in the
domed old barracks are so big that you could fling a
robbit through them anywhere."

The cold quarters, the drills in the snow, and the
coarse food were the cause of much grumbling. Few of
the privates went through these months at Camp Washburn without having their patriotic ardor considerably
cooled. Some wrote complaining letters for publication
in the Grant County Herald. The contrast between
these hardships and the comforts and enjoyments of
home was probably as great in my case as in that of any
one in the company, but I did not suffer my ardor to
cool. Had I done so, my father could have said: "I
told you so."

I made a good many enemies by writing a letter to the Herald, in which I claimed that we were faring sumptuously for soldiers, and that those who grumbled most did not live so well when at home. That was my first effort at getting into print, and I came so near being thrashed for it, that I have never since felt a longing to whack anybody through the columns of a newspaper.

One day we were marched to the city through a driving storm for review. When we had splashed around through slush and mud, and falling rain, and snow, until we had been reviewed and reviewed by some fellows who stood on a covered porch dressed in broadcloth and brass buttons, silk scarfs and plumed hats, we were formed in columns of fours in front of the Newhall House, and there we stood in the snow and rain while the fellows who wore the shoulder straps partook of champagne and like luxuries, within. A sandwich and a cup of coffee had been provided for each of us.

Had the officers fared as the men did, all would have been well. Had there been no storm, it wouldn't have been so bad. My ideas about all men being created free and equal, were badly demoralized on that occasion. For once, I had nothing to say when others grumbled.

Not one of that crowd of officers became distinguished. Hundreds of the privates who stood there in line, are now in everything that goes to make up manhood, head and shoulders above a large majority of those who then wore the shoulder straps. The officers who succeeded best in commanding volunteer American soldiers, were those who roughed it with the men. Who ever heard of Sheridan, or Sherman, or Grant keeping men in line in a storm, while he feasted in a hotel?

My file leader in the company was Horace C. Carr. He was a man of medium height, black hair and eyes, broad across the shoulders and thighs, had long arms, and was knock-kneed. Carr could not learn to keep step. One day when we were drilling, I kicked his heel to remind him that he was out of step. He got mad and threatened to box my ears. I expressed an earnest desire to have him commence at once. Had n't the least doubt in the world that I could beat him in a fight He looked me over in his peculiar, sneering way, and then said:

"Sonny, did you come away to get weaned?"

I afterward found out that there were few, if any, men in the company who could handle Carr, and, notwithstanding this stormy beginning of our acquaintance, Carr afterward became as warm a friend to me as any man ever had.

In March, we were transferred to Benton Barracks, near St. Louis. There we drilled two months more, waiting for arms and horses. In June, having received arms and horses, we were transported on boats to Jefferson City, and from there began our first march, which brought us to Springfield, Mo. Resting there a few days, we started on what, up to that time, was the longest march or raid of the war. This was the march of General Curtis from Springfield to Helena, Arkansas.

At that time, the policy of the Government was to whip the rebels without hurting their feelings. Nothing in the way of forage was to be taken without paying for it. We must pass through the country and leave the growing crops uninjured, leave the slaves there to do the work, leave cattle, hogs, horses and mules; nothing was to be touched or injured unless absolutely required for the subsistence of the army, and even then, vouchers were given. Before starting out on this march, orders were read to the troops in accordance with this government policy. It is needless to say that the private soldiers had more sense. Whenever they heard of a farm that belonged to a rebel in arms, they paid it a visit if they could and took whatever they wanted in the line of forage and provision. Some of the officers tried hard at first to enforce the orders against this foraging. We were commanded to keep in ranks while marching, formed in line and roll called before camping, and then a chain guard was placed around the camp to keep us from getting out. My recollection is that I did not during that march let a day go by without making a raid on my own hook upon the resources of the enemy. I used to slip out of the ranks, get what forage I wanted, then keep the regiment in sight until I saw them halting for camp, when I would slip back as they were forming for roll-call, as that was always a time of confusion.

About the third night out, I got back from my raid too late. The regiment was in camp and guards stationed. I tried to slip in through the brush, but a guard saw and captured me. Tried to divide with him and get off, but he wasn't that kind. He took me to Col. Washburn's tent. I had honey, two hams, some chickens, and some bundles of oats for my horse. These things were all unloaded into the tent, and then the colonel read the riot act. I told him I didn't believe in going hungry or starving my horse, while the rebels, whose country we were in, had plenty. The colonel admitted that he wasn't in love with the government policy himself, but he said that he was under orders, and he would obey whether he liked them or not, and he put it to me whether that wasn't the right thing for every soldier to do. I had to admit that it was. Then he said that if I would promise to ride in the ranks and obey orders thereafter, he would excuse me this time. I promised and I was then permitted to go to my company.

That night when I began to think it over, I regretted having made such a promise. Would just as soon plough corn as ride in the ranks in hot weather over dusty roads. That was one of the hardships of war that I had not counted on. The next morning I told Captain Woods and Lieutenant Riley what had occurred, and that I didn't believe I wanted to be bound by any such agreement. I asked them whether it would do to go to the colonel and take it back. They thought that was the best thing for me to do if I didn't mean to keep the promise; so to the colonel I went. I told him that after thinking it over, I concluded to take back the promise I had made. He was at breakfast, and ham, and chicken, and honey were on his bill of fare. He looked at me a moment, and I could see that his frown had to struggle with a smile, but he managed to look angry as he thundered out: " Go to your company, sir, I will make an example of you. Your impudence is worse than your disobedience." A moment after, our pickets were fired on and we formed in line of battle where we remained all day expecting attack, and I suppose the colonel forgot to fulfill his promise to make an example of me, for I never heard anything more about it.

During this march I got into a quarrel with a big six-footer, and was in a fair way to be well pommeled when Horace Carr interfered. He said to the big fellow: "I aint very large myself, but I am full grown and used to being licked; if you are dying for a fight, let the boy alone and amuse yourself with me." There was no fight, but from that time on Carr and myself were friends.

During the march all of the soldiers supposed the objective point to be Little Rock, and we expected a hard battle there, for we learned from the negroes as we approached that place, that great preparations were being made to receive us. We reached Clarendon, east of Little Rock without any fighting, except now and then a skirmish with guerrillas. There we turned to the east, marched rapidly all night, and went into Helena on the Mississippi. I was one of the advance guard as we charged into the town. Had we been a few minutes earlier, we could have captured the rebel general, Pillow. He was crossing the river on an old flat-boat, and was some distance from the farther shore when we rode up to the bank of the river.

ESCAPE OF GEN. PILLOW.

CHAPTER IV.

HELENA—A SLAVE-OWNER IN A BAD FIX—" FORNINST THE
GOVERNMENT "—PLANTATION RECORDS—MEMPHIS PRO-
HIBITION IN THE ARMY—HELPING A FRIEND TO BEAT
THE QUARTERMASTER.

We remained at Helena from early in July until
late in January. The country back of the town to the
North is high and perhaps healthy. South, East, and
West are the low bottom lands full of swamps and
bayous. The town is on low ground protected by a
levee from overflow. It is, or was then, a sickly hole.
Fever and ague and other diseases which make short
work of a northern man who goes there in July, carried
off at least ten per cent of our regiment.

Helena is in the cotton belt. There were thousands
of negroes on the cotton plantations. The government
was at that time trying to save the Union and slavery
too. The negroes came into Helena by hundreds.
Their masters would follow them in and get permits to
take them back. The privates, many of us were not in
accord with the Government on the negro question.
We used to follow the masters when they started away
with their slaves, release the slaves and convince the
masters that it would be best to keep away from camp.

On one occasion, Carr and I saw a man leave town
with a lot of his negroes who had run away. We followed him out about ten miles and then stopped him.
We sent the negroes back to town, took the master's

A SLAVE OWNER IN A BAD FIX.

horse, and told him to stay out of Helena. Carr asked me to ride back with the negroes, as they were afraid other slave-owners would arrest them, while he would conceal .himself and see if the enraged master would attempt to follow us into camp.

Before I got back to town Carr overtook me leading another captured horse. He absolutely refused to answer any questions, and, fearing that the man had started to follow us back, and that Carr had killed him, I was willing that silence should be maintained. A few weeks after, I saw this slave-owner in town. He wasn't trying to take out negroes any more. I pointed him out to Carr, who then told me what had happened before. He saw the man coming on a horse, waylaid him, took him into the woods and handcuffed his hands around a tall tree and left him there. Carr had found the handcuffs on a plantation where they had been used in disciplining negroes, and he carried them in his saddle-bags as a curiosity; said he left the man near the traveled road so that there would be no question about his being released.

All that summer we carried on a warfare of that kind against what we believed to be the mistaken policy of the government. It had a bad effect on the soldiers. They got to be like Irishmen when they land in New York, "forninst the government." The government tried to protect rebels in their property. The soldier said, "a rebel's property belongs to the government, but if the government won't have it, I will," especially a soldier who was kept where there was no fighting to do.

After a while the boys ceased to make any distinction between captured and other government property. I remember that a boat load of Irish potatoes was unloaded on the wharf at Helena; they were scarce down there, and in great demand. An infantry soldier was on guard over them. We wanted some of those potatoes. That night we borrowed some muskets from infantry men, obtained the countersign, and when the guard at the pile of potatoes had been on duty until his two hours were nearly up, we marched up with a pretended relief guard and relieved him. He went to camp and we carried off potatoes.

Of course, that was wrong, but such acts were frequently committed, without conscientious scruples, by honest men, because they had lost respect for the goverment, on account of the policy that was being pursued. It seemed to us that the government gave more thought and care to the protection of the property and rights of rebels than to the safety and comfort of men who had enlisted to fight for the Union.

While at Helena I was taken with chills and fever. An overseer on one of General Pillow's plantations offered to take me to his house and cure me. I went with him. There had been nearly two hundred negroes on that plantation; not one was left. The government didn't go quite so far as to return runaway negroes to a rebel general and keep them at work. That man and his wife had two sons. They were both in the rebel army. One had been wounded and was taken prisoner. They nursed and doctored me with as much care as they could have bestowed on one of their own boys. It

gave them a feeling of security to have a Union soldier
in their house.

On that plantation I used to read the records kept
by the overseer. It seems that every overseer of a
large plantation kept a daily record. That record
showed that there were negroes whipped, bucked and
gagged, and otherwise punished every day. Every
negro who came from the field with less than his stint
of cotton, received so many lashes. I saw there the
same kind of instruments of torture that I afterward
saw in Andersonville. One machine was rigged for
stretching negroes over a large roller, so that the lash
could be applied to the bare skin. If anyone believes
that the cruelties practised on the slaves were exagger-
ated in Uncle Tom's Cabin, let him hunt up and read
one of those plantation records.

Except a few unimportant raids and a little scouting, we might as well have been infantry men during
all these months at Helena. About February 1st, we
were transported on boats up to Memphis. I rode from
the steamboat out to the camp ground in a storm of sleet
and snow; and before tents were pitched for shelter,
was wet and nearly frozen. Caught a bad cold, which
terminated in pneumonia; was taken to the hospital.
The doctors said my health had been so badly broken
by fever and ague that it would be impossible for me to
survive this attack of pneumonia. Their conclusion
was telegraphed to my parents.

Carr helped to carry me to the hospital and never
left me until I was out of danger. One night when I
had been unconscious for twenty-four hours, it seemed

that I was awakened by some one rubbing my feet. I
could see and hear, but could not move or speak. The
doctor, the steward, and Carr were close to me, and the
doctor said to the others that I would be gone before
morning. When the others went away I managed to
make Carr understand that I was conscious and hungry.
He fed me; I told him I was going to fool that doctor,
and then went to sleep. In the morning, I woke up out
of danger; was able to walk when my mother got there.
She took me to a private boarding-house and staid with
me until I was entirely well.

Soldier life at Memphis was very nearly a repetition of that of Helena. Our camp was surrounded by a -
chain of guards and we were not permitted to go away
from camp without a pass.

Our adventures were chiefly of the disorderly kind.
How to get out of camp, take in the city, and then get
back without being arrested, was the question. I went
to the city three times as often as I would have gone had
there been no camp guard to prevent. The selling of
liquor to soldiers at the saloons, or by anyone, was forbidden. Before that order was issued, I seldom thought
of drinking anything. After the order was issued, I
never went into the city without finding a place where
the order could be evaded. Such rules and orders have
that effect on most young men. When we were at
Helena, rations of whisky were issued to us, and half of
the soldiers wouldn't touch it. Most all of them who
refused whisky at Helena, drank every time they could
get anything to drink at Memphis.

The regiment went out on one raid before I was

able to ride. Carr brought back a captured horse. He bought it from another man who captured it. The men who captured horses and mules always sold them if they could. The regimental quartermaster always confiscated all such property if he could. Between him and the soldiers there was continual strife. Carr expected to get out of the ranks with his purchase before getting back to camp, but he was so closely watched that he could not. Early the next morning the quartermaster was around taking a list of captured property, and of course he put down Carr's horse. He had a particular grudge against myself and Carr because we had so often outwitted him.

I was at that time permitted to ride where I pleased, because I had not yet been reported fit for duty. The horses were all taken every morning and evening through the city to the river to water. Each man rode one horse and led another. An officer went in charge of each company, and he had to bring back as many men and horses as he took out. The officer of the guard counted them out and in. Carr led his purchase out at watering call. I desired to help him if possible, so I rode out afterward and overtook the watering party. I told Carr to get in the rear coming back from the river. I took the saddle off from my horse and left it at a stable; got on bareback. Watching for a chance when the column returning from the river turned a corner in the city, and the officer in charge could not see the rear of his company, I rode my horse quickly in between the one Carr rode and the one he led, slipped from my horse on to the other, and Carr took my horse

back to camp. That made the count all correct. I left
Carr's horse at a stable, got into a hack and was driven
to the camp, and was in Captain Woods' tent when the
men and horses returned.

The quartermaster soon came in swearing mad, and
required Captain Woods to produce the captured horse.
The captain was not friendly to Carr, and he entered
with great zeal into the search for the missing horse.
The officer that had been to the river declared that
Carr brought back the horse he took to water. Some
of the boys knew better, but they wouldn't give us away.
That let Carr out. Then the quartermaster accused
me on general principles. The captain declared that I
was writing in his tent when the men came back with
the horses, and he knew I did n't have anything to do
with it. Then he said to the quartermaster: "That
horse was hitched to the picket-rope this morning when
you listed him, and if you have let some one take him
away in broad daylight, do n't you blame me for it."

I always made out the pay-rolls for the company,
and had been at work on them that morning in the captain's tent. I went back to work; the captain came in.
He looked at me awhile, and then said: "Melvin, how
did you manage to get that horse out of camp?" I told
him all about it; never attempted to conceal anything
from either Captain Woods or Lieutenant Riley, and
neither of them would catch me doing anything wrong
if he could possibly avoid it. Carr sold his horse so as
to clear $40.

CHAPTER V.

In May we were transported in boats down to
Vicksburg and up the Yazoo river to Hains' Bluff.
There we went into camp to help watch Johnson who
was waiting for a chance to raise the siege. We had
something to do there; raiding, and scouting parties out
every day. Once we crossed the Yazoo, and made a
raid into the Running Water country. We captured
a large herd of cattle and some prisoners and horses. I .
captured a fine young mare. An officer of the 7th Kansas
cavalry offered to give me $60 if I would bring the mare
to his camp without letting her get branded. When the
quartermaster once got his U. S. brand on a horse's
shoulder, no one would buy.

When we got to the river on our return, the brigade
quartermaster was there to take charge of all the captured property. He stood on the steam ferry-boat as
the horses were loaded for crossing, and permitted no
horse to go on board without the U. S. brand. I took
in the situation while another regiment was being
ferried. Then I chewed the end of a stick into a brush,
got some tar from the hub of an old-fashioned wagon,
and made U. S. with tar on my captured horse; worked
the tar well into the hair, then rubbed it off with sand

until I had a fine brand.   I had to tell my captain what
I was up to, as each captain was required to stand at the
gang-plank to assist the quartermaster as his company
went on board.   I took my horse on first, and then went
back and brought up the rear with my captured mare.
The captain managed to move away as I led the mare
up the plank, and the " U. S." was so plain that no questions were asked.

When our regiment was alone or at the head of a
column during a raid, my company was in advance of
the regiment. A boy named Lynn Cook, and myself,
nearly always rode as videttes or scouts, in advance of
the advance guard.   I do n't remember how it came
about, but this place was always accorded to Cook and
myself, probably because we had keen eyes and good
horses, and never failed to discover the enemy.

We had skirmishes with Johnson's cavalry almost
every day. One day the patrol guard went out, under
Lieutenant Showalter—twelve or fifteen men, Cook and
myself being advance guards. We saw three rebels
coming toward us. We supposed them to be the advance, as they were, of a larger party. Without having been seen, we rode back and reported, and asked
the lieutenant to let us hide in a fence corner and capture the Johnnies. He would not, but formed us in
line on the side of the road where the rebels could n't
possibly get nearer than one hundred yards without
seeing us.

They came riding carelessly along, one of them
sitting sideways on his horse. We were all ready, and
when they caught sight of us the lieutenant said, "fire."

Not a man was touched, but as they wheeled to run, the one sitting sideways was knocked off and captured.

I was riding a little race horse that had been captured at Fort Pillow. He had both speed and endurance, but he would n't stand fire. On this occasion, as soon as the volley was fired, he bolted with me and dashed after the two rebels that were running away. They had a hundred yards the start, but in less than a quarter of a mile I was within a few rods of them. I had been trying all the time to stop my horse, and only managed to pull him up when about to run into a whole company of rebels that came dashing up the road to support their advance. Had the two Johnnies who supposed I was chasing them, not been in the way, I should certainly have been shot by the others. My horse once turned, carried me swifty back, nor did I try to hold him.

Immediately after the surrender of Vicksburg we crossed the Big Black river, and started in pursuit of Johnson's army. I never could understand why Sherman did not crush Johnson at Jackson. I was detailed as an orderly for General Parkes, who commanded the 9th corps. The 9th corps was on our left. There was some fighting. I rode back and forth along our lines every day carrying messages, and could see that the rebels were withdrawing, leaving only a skirmish line behind their breast-works. In company with a man from the signal corps, I went on top of the insane asylum with Gen. Parkes' field glass, and reported to him what was going on. The rebels saw us and fired at us with cannon, regardless of consequences to the in-

THE CHARGE OF A RUNAWAY HORSE.

sane. Then I climbed a tall tree from which I could see the movements of the enemy. They were evacuating the city all day, and I never could understand why, when one half had crossed the river, the other was not gobbled up.

The day after Jackson was taken, our regiment went on a raid to Canton. Some rebels came out to meet us. They formed in line in the edge of some woods, and we formed in a field just out of reach of them, and there we waited until they moved away. Why we didn't have a fight there, I never could see.

We camped that night at a little place called Vernon. In an abandoned house I found a trunk addressed to Captain —— of a rebel regiment; broke it open, and among other things that were evidently intended for a soldier in camp, there was a pair of fine woolen blankets and a little bag of silver. These I took. I presented the blankets to our colonel, Stevens, and kept the silver, four or five dollars.

A few days after that, Uncle Tommy, as the boys called the colonel, got on his ear because so many of us left the ranks to forage. Had he kept us where there was fighting to do, he would have had no trouble, but fighting was n't in his line, and we all knew it. I had been scouting on my own hook one day, and, on coming to camp, found a camp-guard out. Not expecting anything of the kind, I was captured and taken before Colonel Stevens. He was in a great rage. Had my forage, of which I had a load, taken from me, and ordered me to get off my horse and be searched. I told him I had not taken anything but forage, and was not in the habit of taking anything else. Adjutant Scott asked to see what I had in my pockets.   As the colonel, who was a rank Englishman, saw the silver, he fairly frothed at the mouth.

"Where di 'e get that?"

" In a house at Vernon," I replied.

" Been a burnin' 'ouses 'ave 'e, been a robbin' of people and burnin' 'ouses, 'ave 'e? I'll teach 'e to break horders and burn 'ouses, so I will. Hadjutant, send this man to his company under harrest."

I tried to explain but he ordered me off. Lieutenant Riley saw Adjutant Scott next morning, and together they pacified the colonel.   Nothing further would have been said or done had I been content to let the matter rest.   The colonel called me hard names, had taken money from me that he had no better right to than I had, and, as I did not have much respect for him anyway, the more I thought of it the more I thought I had been mis-used.

Examining the army regulations, I found that valuables taken from the enemy should be turned over to the hospital department.   From Adjutant Scott I learned that the colonel had kept my silver and made no report of it. After talking the matter over with Captain Woods, who was then acting as major, I concluded to ask the colonel for the silver. So one day when we had halted for a noon-day rest, I walked up to the colonel, who was lying in the shade surrounded by other officers, and asked him to return the silver that he had taken from me.   He reached for his sabre, jumped up and made for me as though he meant to run me through on the spot. Captain Woods and the other officers stopped him and reminded him that he had no right to use his sabre on a soldier for asking a question.

A few weeks after this, we were in camp near Vicksburg and orders came from Washington to grant furloughs for meritorious conduct to two soldiers in each company. My conduct had not been in all respects meritorious, but I had, on several occasions, volunteered for hazardous service, and had never been known to shirk when there was dangerous work to do. I was one of the two recommended by the officers of my company for furlough. I had never had or asked for a furlough, and now to get one for meritorious conduct, and visit my home in the North during the hot, sickly weather when the army would be idle, nothing could have pleased me more.

Imagine my feelings when the recommendation came back disapproved by Colonel Stevens. I went with Captain Wood to see him. We had a stormy interview. The colonel said I deserved a court-martial rather than a furlough. The captain then demanded a court-martial.

I was subsequently tried before a court-martial on charges preferred by Colonel Stevens. The trial was in the colonel's tent. I did not hear the evidence submitted against me, but I was called in and asked to explain how and where I obtained the silver, and why I asked the colonel to return it to me. I sat on a cot in the colonel's tent, and turning up the blankets, noticed the very same white blankets that I took from the trunk in which I found the silver. When I had told where I got the silver, I said:

"Gentlemen, I took a pair of white wool blankets from the same trunk and presented them to Colonel Stevens. He thanked me with great kindness and made no inquiries as to where I got them. I think these are the same blankets."

I uncovered a pair of white blankets on the cot. The officers of the court smiled; the colonel got red in the face and tried to explain, but about all that he could say was that he did not know that I was the boy that gave him the blankets. As I never heard anything more from the court-martial, I suppose that the charges were not sustained.

I liked my companions in the company and never had any trouble with my company officers, but, knowing that the colonel was watching for a chance to get me into trouble, and fearing that he might, I obtained through Captain Woods an order from the division commander, placing me on detached service, and assigning me for duty at the division headquarters in Vicksburg. There I was an orderly for two or three months and was then made chief of orderlies.

The duties of an orderly in an army that is in actual service are about the same as those of a page in Congress. The orderlies usually know everything and see everything that is going on. If they please the officers under whom they work they are well treated, if they do not, they are sent to their regiment.

My duties at the division headquarters, especially

after I was promoted to chief of orderlies, were light and pleasant. I would in all probability have remained on detached service until the term for which I enlisted expired, had I not met with the misfortune hereafter related.

CHAPTER VI.

In February, 1864, my regiment was in camp at
Redbone Church, twelve miles south of Vicksburg,
Major Harry Eastman, in command. The weather
was delightful, the regiment in good health and fine
spirits. Dashing Harry, as the major was sometimes
called, and nearly all of his officers and men, were
reported to be coining money in the cotton business.
Every man that I saw in the regiment reported "jolly
good times in camp."

There was not much to do at division headquarters.
General McArthur and most of the men in the division
were out on the Meridian campaign. I obtained from
the adjutant-general a leave of absence for ten days,
and went out to camp to have some fun with the boys.

The cotton camp was on the Black River, several
miles from the main camp at Redbone. From this
camp a raiding party was sent out nearly every day,
avowedly for the purpose of hunting Whittaker's
scouts, a band of guerillas that infested the region,
but really for the purpose of protecting teams that
followed after to bring in cotton. The first morning after
I arrived at the cotton camp a raiding party one hundred
strong started out under Dashing Harry himself. I

went along and, being a visitor and not obliged to stay
in the ranks, I soon discovered the object of the raid.
At every plantation the major would have a private
interview with the planter and then march on. As
soon as the command was fairly out of sight that
planter would have all the hands on the place hitching
up teams and loading on cotton. We started at an
early hour; about noon we reached Port Gibson, and
went in on a charge, scaring the people out of their
wits and causing the few daring rebels that were there
to see the girls they had left behind them to leave
with short allowance. Here I enlisted four of the
boys, whom I considered of good grit, into a scheme to
gobble a team and load of cotton. Our plan was to
slip out when the command was about ready to start,
remain in town until the rest were out of sight, then
secure a team, load it with cotton, and follow the command into camp. All went well until the troops began
to disappear over the hill, then five of us seemed a
small number to hold the town, and before the rear
guard had disappeared over the hill three of my boys
deserted, leaving two of us in Port Gibson. Night was
coming on by the time we were fairly out of town with
our four mule team and negro driver. At one of the
plantations where I had seen the major interview the
planter we halted, and ordered him to load that team
with cotton as soon as possible. He asked who I
wanted the cotton for. I told him for Major Eastman.
He had that team loaded in less than a jiffy. We left
the plantation at dark; I rode ahead of the team and
my companion brought up the rear. Our road lay

over a hilly country, part of the way through timber. It was twenty-five miles to camp; the darkness intense. Reader, try such a ride on such a night in a guerilla region, and if you don't wish for the end of your journey before you find it, your experience will not be what mine was. At daybreak we unloaded four bales among other bales of cotton on the bank of the Black River, reported the fact to an officer, and in a few days afterwards Charley Campbell and I received $90 each for our share of that night's work. I afterward saw the planter in Major Eastman's tent, but how they settled for the four bales of cotton I never inquired. Such incidents were the every-day occurrences of the cotton camp.

A few days after this Lieutenant D. L. Riley, with a detachment of men, was sent further up the river to guard a ford, and also to keep the guerillas in that vicinity from molesting the planters as they hauled their cotton to market at Vicksburg.

After establishing his camp at the ford, the lieutenant rode into Redbone. He told me that he had learned from a negro that there was a large quantity of C. S. A. cotton (cotton purchased by the confederate government and branded C.S.A.) concealed in a swamp six or seven miles above his camp at the ford. I returned with Riley and found Lieutenant Showalter and the men very much excited. During the night a large band of guerillas had charged up to the opposite bank of the river and fired on them—but as all the boys were sleeping behind bales of cotton, none were hurt. That day we scouted in all directions but could hear nothing of the guerillas, though we saw a number of men that looked as though they might do good service. As each one had a surgeon's certificate exempting him from conscription, and also professed loyalty to the Union, we passed them by. There was one, however, a fine looking man of thirty or thereabouts, that particularly excited the lieutenant's suspicion. He not only showed a surgeon's certificate, but also a pass and a letter from the post commander at Vicksburg. I think his name was Warner.

The next morning in company with Sergeant E. Wiseman, Lynn B. Cook, H. C. Carr, James Shanley, George Cornish, Patrick Woods, and James Johnson, I crossed the river, intending to make a circuit through the country, and come to the river at the swamp above where the C. S. A. cotton was reported to be. It was our intention to make a raft of the cotton and float it down the river to camp. We started before daybreak; I was riding ahead and out of sight of the rest of the party, when I came in sight of the plantation, owned by the fine-looking, suspicious gentleman before mentioned, just in time to see him dismount at his gate and lead his horse toward the house. I put spurs to the mule that I was riding, and when I reached the house the man had unsaddled the horse, a fine looking animal, and was holding him by the bridle. I rode up, revolver in hand, and asked him where he had been so early in the morning. He replied that a lady in the house had been taken sick in the night and he had been to see a physician. I told him that I had been compelled to ride a mule because my horse was sick, and that I would be obliged to take his horse; but that if he would come to camp that night, he might have his horse back if the lieutenant was willing.   He made some remonstrances and spoke of a letter of protection from some Union officer.   I dismounted with the intention of putting my saddle on the horse, but just then a lady stepped on the porch, and the man gave her the bridle saying:

"If you take this horse, you must take it from the owner."

She said: "You Yankees have taken everything I had in the world except this horse, and if you get this you will have to take it from me by force !"

I supposed the lady to be the wife of the man. Both had an air of gentility and used the language of culture.   My ideas of chivalry did not admit of my taking a horse from a lady by force, and so I vented my spleen on the man in threats and insulting language, mounted my mule and rode away.   We arrived at Hankinson's ferry, just below the cotton, about nine o'clock.   Four of the party went to see if the cotton was all right and four of us remained at the house to have breakfast prepared for all.   The inmates of the house were the ferryman, his wife, and an old negress. The house, itself, was one of the double log houses common in the South, the two parts of the house being separated, the space between, called the "passage," having floor and roof but no side walls.   The house fronted the river; the road, leading from it, ran up the river.

The old auntie prepared the breakfast and called us in.   We sat down to the table.   One of our number was a handsome young man, then about 23 years of age. At his country home he had been the pet and pride of the family; a leader among the young folks of his neighborhood. He was active, witty, and clever In our company he had been, from the first, a kind of clown or fun-maker. Sometimes he would play drunk, get arrested, and carried struggling and kicking before some officer, where, to the chagrin of his captors, he would stand up sober as a judge. His favorite role was that of a camp-meeting preacher. His parents were Methodists, and his store of the words and phrases peculiar to camp-meeting and revival sermons was indeed wonderful. Mounted on a box, barrel, or stump, he would go through an entire camp-meeting service—song, sermon, prayer and all—and so perfectly could he act his part that strangers were often astonished to learn that he was merely in jest.

On this occasion we were no sooner seated around the table than this young man, assuming perfect gravity of manner, bowed his head and pretended to invoke the Divine blessing. The old auntie opened wide her eyes with astonishment, and, at the conclusion "Thank God," she said, "de Yankees am not all sinnas."

Poor boy! How little he thought he was never again to take a seat at a well-spread table, and that the memory of that blessing, asked in mockery, would haunt him to his grave. It did haunt him to his dying hour and he died of hunger. Often afterward, half-naked, cold and sick and nearly famished for food, as he took his poor ration of bread, the memory of that thoughtless mimicry would come over him and the

tears of bitter remorse would chase each other down
his bony cheeks.   Boys, if you are ever tempted to
scoff at sacred things let this poor boy's fate be a warning.   His thoughtless act was not the cause of his early
death, but, done as it was, an instant before an un-
expected crisis, it made a deep and lasting impression,
and none can say what his future might have been but
for the influence of that guilty feeling on his mind.   No
man knows what an hour, even a moment, may bring
forth.   Remember this from Burns:

> The great Creator to revere,
>   Must sure become the creature;
> But still the preaching cant forbear,
>   And ev'n the rigid feature ;
> Yet ne'er with wits profane to range
>   Be complaisance extended ;
> An atheist's laugh's a poor exchange
>   For Deity offended.
>
> When ranting round in pleasure's ring
>   Religion may be blinded;
> Or if she gie a random sting,
>   It may be little minded;
> But when in life we're tempest driv'n,
>   A conscience but a canker,—
> A correspondence fixed with Heaven
>   Is sure a noble anchor.

We had just commenced to eat, when some dogs
began barking around the house.   Sergeant Wiseman
went out and came in directly, saying there was a man
on the other side of the river calling for the ferry, and
that he would stay out and stand guard until the rest
of us had finished our breakfast.   I was just rising from
the table, when there burst upon our ears the unearthly
hip, hip, hip, of the rebel yell. I leaped into the passage
to grab a gun, and whiz, whiz, whiz, the bullets flew all
around me.   I thought of the corn-field, and looked
that way; a line of rebels was within a hundred yards.

Turning toward the gate, the muzzles of a half dozen cocked guns were leveled at me. Instantly and almost instinctively my hands went up in token of surrender, and I hastened toward the men in front, to escape being shot by those behind.

As before stated, I had been acting as chief of orderlies at division headquarters, and was, therefore, in better dress than private soldiers usually wear. My only weapon was an elegant silver mounted self-cocking revolver, fastened around me by a morocco belt, such as officers usually wore. I had, being so ordered in no gentle words, unbuckled this belt and was handing it with revolver attached, up to the man nearest me who sat on his horse, when I saw coming toward me, his face pale with rage and shot-gun in hand, the man, Warner, riding the very same horse that his sister had kept me from taking a few hours before. It was well that I saw him and that my presence of mind did not forsake me. I knew from the expression on his face and his actions as well, that he was ready to shoot me, but could not, where I stood, without danger to the man to whom I was handing the belt.

As the man took the belt and revolver, I saw that he was pleased with it. Such weapons were highly prized by the rebels, and I quickly handed up my watch and pocketbook, and said as I did so:

"Am I your prisoner?"

"Well, I reckon! How big are them boots?" he said.

"You can have the boots, but don't let that man shoot me," I quickly responded.

Looking at Warner Boatwright, for that was my captor's name, said:

"What in hell are you pointing your gun at this Yank, for? He is my prisoner."

"I do n't care a damn whose prisoner he is, I am going to shoot him," said Warner.

It seemed that these men were not personally asquainted, for Boatwright's reply was something like this:

"I reckon you do n't know me, by G—d, I'm Boatwright, the independent scout, that's who I am; and when any man shoots my prisoner, he had better shoot me first."

More words followed back and forth, until finally Boatwright moved his horse away from me, and with cocked revolver in hand, said to Warner:

"You are going to kill that unarmed boy, are you? Now you just blaze away!"

Warner knew what that flashing eye and defiant manner meant, and, completely cowed, he turned his horse and rode away. Is it any wonder that I remember almost every act and word of those two men during those few brief moments, or any wonder that I remember nothing else of what was going on around? I had watched and listened to that quarrel fully realizing that my life was wavering in the balance. Warner, because, perhaps, he was not cool enough in such an emergency to invent a story better suited to his purpose, had related our morning encounter about as it was. I admitted what he said, and claimed that he had not sufficient provocation to justify his shooting me; and so Boat-

"WHAT IN H——L ARE YOU POINTING YOUR GUN AT THIS YANK FOR?"   HE'S MY PRISONER."

wright thought. Warner's real reason for wanting to
put me out of the way, was, no doubt, because he knew
I had seen his surgeon's certificate, and his permit to go
and come through the Union lines, and now here he was
in arms with rebels, and therefore liable to be shot as a
spy should he be caught and tried. But these things
came up and were talked over later in the day. No
more was said up to the time Warner rode away, than
I before stated, and not until he had gone, did I feel
the terrible strain. Then I weakened, my knees knocked
together as though an ague chill was on me, and I had
to sit down to keep from falling.

Meantime, while these things that I remember so
well were transpiring, the rest of the boys were being
captured, and the plunder, consisting of horses, guns,
revolvers, watches, money, and whatever they had
worth taking, was being divided between twenty-five or
thirty guerillas, in whose hands we now were. Except-
ing Boatwright, and one or two others who claimed to
be independent scouts, they belonged to Whittaker's
scouts.

But all this time, where is Sergeant Wiseman, who
went out to stand guard? Some of the guerillas said
they had fired at a man crawling up the bank on the
other side of the river. Those of us who were taken,
supposed that he saw the guerillas approaching, and
without giving us any alarm, sought his own safety in
flight. I have never heard his account of the affair and
can, therefore, only hope that we were wrong.

CHAPTER VII.

Just after Warner rode away, and while the remainder of our captors were arranging to follow, we
were all startled by the report of a gun from the other
side of the river and the whistling of a bullet directly
over our heads. Looking in the direction from which
the sound came, we saw James Trelore, one of our company, taking his carbine from his shoulder, as he did so,
he wheeled his horse and galloped away. Several
shots were fired at him by our guardians, none of which
took effect.

It seems that he had been sent up to see how we
were getting along, and that he had arrived on the
other side of the river just in time to see us in the
hands of our new friends. Trelore was a good shot
and I have always supposed that he did not aim closely
at any of the rebels for fear of hitting us, but merely
fired over their heads with a view of frightening them
away. They did not frighten, and he came near paying
dearly for his audacity.

Out of the twenty-five or thirty guerillas that surrounded us in the first place, only five or six remained
after our capture was made, the rest galloped away on
the trail of the other four of our party. They came

upon them in the woods and a sharp skirmish ensued,
resulting in the wounding of Carr in the thigh by a
buckshot and the killing of one of the guerilla horses.
The guerillas, after exchanging a few shots at long
range, and finding that there were only four, charged on
them with the usual rebel yell. Carr, too brave for his
own good, took deliberate aim at short range and would
have killed his man had not the horse's head, suddenly
raised, received the bullet. Before he could re-charge
his carbine, a dozen men were around him. Bringing
their prisoners together, the guerillas rode away with
us rapidly until about the middle of the afternoon, when
we came to the rendezvous, where we found Captain
Whittaker and the rest of his band.

Here Warner demanded of the captain that I be
delivered over to him as his prisoner to be dealt with
as he might see fit, at the same time stating his reasons
for the demand. Boatwright spoke up boldly and
charged that Warner had been afraid to show his colors
in the morning when I had met him single-handed, and
that he now wanted to take me off and murder me after
I had been made a prisoner by others. He intimated
very strongly, too, that he had promised me his protection, and that it wouldn't be safe for Warner or any
one else to harm a hair of my head.

The quarrel between the two men again waxed
warm, and it transpired that Warner's real reason for
wanting to put me out of the way was not so much what
I had said and done that morning as the fact that I had
seen his pass from a Union officer, and could, should I
escape, or in any other way get back into the Union

army, and cause his capture, furnish evidence to convict him as a spy. Whittaker listened awhile and then decided in this way:

"Young man," he said to me, "I don't think you have done anything very much out of the way, but unless you will take an oath that you will never, under any circumstances, seek revenge on Warner, or try to do him harm, I shall turn you over to him to do with as he sees fit."

I saw no other way out, but I think I made some mental reservations as I held up my hand and took that oath. If my memory serves me right, all of my fellow-prisoners were required to take the same oath.

Even then, Warner was not satisfied. He asked to be one of the number detailed to guard us. To this, Boatwright vigorously objected, and volunteered to be one of our guards himself, for the purpose, as he plainly stated, of seeing that Warner did not play the sneak and get a shot at an unarmed foe.

Boatwright was certainly a generous and brave man. He told us some wonderful stories of his exploits as a scout and guerilla, some of which if true, were not to his credit; but his whole conduct while with us, indicated, that though rough in appearance and coarse in language, he had anything but a mean spirit.

·   If I remember correctly, there were seven guards in all, under command of Boatwright; who started with us for the headquarters of the rebel general in command of that district. The first night we camped where there were two log cabins. We were put into one, the guards took the other. Two at a time stood guard at our door.

Carr and I arranged a plan for our escape. We proposed that when all the guards but the two were asleep, we would suddenly spring on these two, get their guns and capture the rest before they could be aroused, and then by traveling in the night only, and through the woods, go with the prisoners to our own lines. It was a feasible plan, and at first all agreed to it. But as the time for action approached, two or three of the boys became faint-hearted and declared it should not be done. So they shut the door and laid down in front of it, threatening that they would cry out and alarm the guard, should any of us attempt to open the door.

Thus securely guarded both by friends and foes, I spent my first night as a prisoner. The boys that refused to join in the break for liberty were probably right. They said they were afraid it could not be done without killing some of the guards, and that whether any of them were hurt or not, we could not take so large a party back to our lines without discovery and re-capture, and that if we tried and failed, we would all be shot.

The second night we came to the camp of a rebel brigade—these were regular rebel soldiers—they treated us well. Gave us a tent to sleep in, plenty to eat, and two of us, Cook and myself, and two of the Johnnies, as we called them, engaged in a friendly game of draw-poker during the greater part of the night. Neither Cook nor myself had any money, but some of the Johnnies, just to see the fun of the game between two Yanks and two Johnnies, furnished us with funds. We came out ahead, and our backers generously divided with us our winnings.

Here we were placed under charge of new guards, the old ones, except Boatwright, going back. We traveled to Morrisville that day and there waited for a train. By this time, the wound received by Carr had become inflamed and made him sick. Boatwright took him to a physician who examined the wound and said the bullet must be extracted, but before he would do it, he wanted to know where he was to get his pay. Carr told him that he was a prisoner and had no money. Still the physician refused to perform the operation without pay. I mention this as an example of the boasted southern chivalry. Finally, Cook and myself produced the money won in the poker game, and gave it to the man, who then performed the operation and dressed the wound quite skilfully.

We witnessed another illustration of southern chivalry at the same town. We were guarded in a negro quarter or hut. Our supper was brought in by a good-looking mulatto girl. The owner of the place, the girl's master, came in while we were eating, and seemed desirous of arguing with us the questions that divided the North and South.

" You uns," said he, "think a nigger just as good as a white man, don't you?"

"Yes, in some respects," we said.

"Now, I suppose you would just as soon marry a nigger wench as to marry a white woman, wouldn't you?"

Thinking the old gentleman would take a joke, I said to him:

" I wouldn't like to marry any nigger wench that I

have seen around here, for fear that I would have some of you rebels for a daddy-in-law."

As I spoke I looked from him to the mulatto girl, standing near. Whoopee! How the old man did rave! He stormed and swore and finally started for the house saying, he would n't stand such an insult from no damned Yankee. He meant business, too, for he soon came back with a shot gun, which he would doubtless have fired into us, had not Boatwright stood in the door, and, partly by the influence of his drawn revolver and partly by persuasion, appeased the old man's wrath. I was always careful after that about joking with Johnnies.

From this place, we were taken on the cars to Brookhaven, Boatwright still in command of the party. While on the cars, a tall, awkward, loud-mouthed, and vile-tongued man in dirty uniform, commenced to talk and banter with some of our boys. Not getting the best of a wordy engagement, he soon had his six-shooter out and valorously flourishing it in the faces of unarmed prisoners, swore he could whip any five Yanks on earth, and dared any man there to deny it. He had a bottle of liquor with him which he began to drink, and the more he drank the braver he became until he began to talk about killing one Yank, just to celebrate the day. He carried this so far as to order us to draw lots for the honor of being his target. His order not being obeyed, he cocked his weapon and flourished it so recklessly that Boatwright, who until then had scarcely noticed him, leveled a cocked revolver at him and ordered him to lay down his gun. For a moment he looked at the cold, gray eyes behind the cocked revolver, and then began with: " How are ye, pard?" to try and make friends with Boatwright.

"I am no pard of a man that insults prisoners," said Boatwright, and he took the pistol from the cowardly ruffian, uncapped it, threw his bottle of liquor out of the window, and ordered him to take a seat and hold his tongue, which the tall son of chivalry, completely cowed, seemed glad to do.

At Brookhaven, very much to our regret, Boatwright left us. He seemed to have the right to go where he pleased as an independent scout, as he called himself. I know of no reason for his staying with us as long as he did, except to prevent Warner from following us and seeking an opportunity to wreak his vengeance on myself. In fact, he often spoke of his fears on that point, and after the first night until he left us, always insisted upon my sleeping with him. One night while we were at Morrisville, he took Lynn Cook and myself to a tavern, and we all occupied the same room. Before going to bed, he asked us to pledge our word of honor to make no attempt to escape, and then undressed and went to bed with us. He told us he would be very glad to have us get away and safely back to our friends, but he did n't want us to escape while he was in charge of us, for that would cause him trouble.

Just before he left us I had a long talk with him, and he advised me to get away. He gave me all the points he could about the best course to pursue in case I should escape. We saw him go with great reluctance. Although he told of many exploits in killing Union

men and negroes, many of which, if true, were ex-
tremely cruel and not to his credit, his whole treatment
of our party was a splendid example of real chivalry.
I have never seen or heard of him since, but whether he
got killed in some dare-devil venture or, as such men
were likely to do, became a member of some gang of
desperadoes after the war, such as the James Brothers'
gang, I warrant that for personal coolness and nerve
he seldom, if ever, met his superior; and, whatever his
lot, if he still lives, I would be glad and proud to shake
the hand of Boatwright and thank him again for his
kind and manly treatment.

At Brookhaven, Cook, Carr, and myself laid many
plans for escape. Our schemes for getting away by
stealth were all in one way or another frustrated. Some
of them, we thought, by the treachery of our companions. We had joined a larger party of prisoners,
and there were now twenty-five or thirty of us in all.
If we could have united the whole party in an attempt,
we could easily have set ourselves at liberty by force.
But the majority were afraid to try it, claiming that the
whole village and country around would be in arms and
that we would be tracked by blood-hounds and either
killed or re-captured.

We were well treated. In fact a few of us, especially
Lynn Cook and Wm. Cook, who could play on the
fiddle, and myself and one or two other men, had some
regular jollifications. Some of our guards, who were
strangers in the town, formed the acquaintance of the
young folks and got up dancing parties. The ladies
being largely in the majority, because the young men

were all away in the army, some of us Yanks were invited to the parties as the rebel girls said, just to fill up the sets. We fancied that they found our company quite as agreeable as that of any of the Johnnies.

At one of these dancing parties to which Lynn Cook and myself were invited and taken under guard, we made an unsuccessful attempt to escape. It was a warm evening and the windows in the room were up. We arranged a cotillion in which our two guards and ourselves were the gentlemen. We confided our scheme to two of the ladies with whom we had become familiar and to whom we were pretending to make love and they agreed to assist. After the cotillion ended, we called for a waltz, and while our two guards were waltzing and only one guard with a gun left at the front door, our partners were to continue the waltz together and let Lynn and myself slip out of the window. The room was but dimly lighted with one or two tallow candles. Cook went first, had cleared the window, and I was half out, when both our partners screamed: "They are getting away. The Yanks are getting away." The guards seized their guns, ran out at the front door, and, as it was a bright moonlight night, we thought the chances were against us and made as great speed in getting back into the room as we had tried to make in getting out.

Whether our lady friends meant to play us a trick or whether they saw we were noticed by others and screamed to keep themselves from being implicated, we never found out, for we were taken at once to our prison house without being permitted, as formerly, to go home with our girls with guards behind us. We were not invited to any more dances.

A few days after we were taken on the cars back to Morrisville, and from there on foot through Jackson, (which place we helped to capture but a few months before,) to Canton, another town that we had before been in sight of but had not entered, there being, in the opinion of our commander, too many rebels there at the time. As we were all cavalry men and not used to walking, this journey in warm weather, over a sandy road, was hard on our feet. I nearly gave out the first day, and I well remember how glad I was when the rebel guards said that we would camp at a plantation we were approaching.

On nearing the place I recognized the house as one that I had been in on my return trip from Canton, before mentioned. On that occasion, I rode up to this house and found it full of Union soldiers, who were literally stripping it. They were even taking jewelry from the hands of the women. It was customary on such excursions for the officer in command to place guards at such houses to protect them from pillage and the women from insult. Seeing no guard at this house and cowardly work going on, I drew my sword, declared that I was a detailed guard, drove the plunderers away, and staid there until the rear guard came along. The ladies were at the time loud in their praise and profuse in their thanks.

Now, as I neared the same house, tired, limping on blistered feet, and hungry, I thought to myself and probably said to my companions, "we will be well-treated here, because these people owe me a good turn."

The place belonged to Doctor Lee. He came out as we reached the house and the sergeant in charge told him that he desired to camp for the night, and asked whether he could have shelter and food for his men and prisoners. The doctor was all excitement in a moment.

"Food for those damned Yankee thieves?" said he. "I'd feed a hungry dog, but not a damned crumb will I give to a thieving Yankee. If I could see them burning in hell, not a damned drop would I give them to drink. I'll give them shelter, damn them, yes, take them to the nigger quarters. They say a nigger is as good as a white man. I say a nigger is a damn sight better than a white Yankee, and the nigger quarter is too good for them."

This, and much more, he rattled off. Who could blame him? The negro quarters were, as he said, empty, because the Yankees had stolen the negroes away. And what must be the feelings of any husband and father to return to his home and find that armed men had been there and stripped the premises of every living and eatable thing, insulted his wife and daughters, wantonly destroyed what they could not use, and even robbed women of their finger rings. Such had been this man's experience. Who could blame him for his wrath?

Still, I did not then think of it in that light. I induced one of the guards to go and tell him that I was the man that had driven the other Yankees out of his house, and stood guard over the ladies to protect them from further wrong. I felt confident that when he heard this he would invite me at least into his house, and treat me with hospitality. But not so. He sent back an insulting message, and the sergeant said that he refused to allow any of the prisoners to have a mouthful of food while on his place. It was now my turn to get angry, at least, angry I got, and painfully angry, too. In all my life I don't think I have ever at any other time been so completely soaked and choaked with passion as I was at that place. The more I thought of the miserable return I was receiving for the generous action I had performed the more my blood seemed to boil. My feet were painfully blistered. The sergeant had an old negro bring me some water in a tub in which to bathe them. To this old negro I told how I had been there before, and what I had done, and he went away saying he would try and get me something to eat. After an hour or so he came back with a large pan of corn bread and some meat. By this time my indignation had mastered my hunger, and I gave the food to my companions, telling them that if they wanted to eat on that man's place they could, but as for me I wanted no food that he could call his. I lay awake nearly, if not quite, all night, studying how to best take revenge on this Doctor Lee, as soon as I could get free. It turned out that my blood had plenty of time to cool before I got free.

CHAPTER VIII.

On our arrival at Canton we were drawn up in line
before the tent of Colonel Lee. We were told that he
was related to Gen. R. E. Lee Here we were searched
and our names taken on the roll, and we were then sent
to the prison room, which was in the second story of a
large brick building.

Here we found about 150 other prisoners; the room,
as I remember it, was about 25x80 feet. There was in
it a common box heating stove with one lid on top On
this stove the cooking for the whole party was done.
The rations were corn meal and bacon.

There being now nearly, if not quite, 200 men in the
room you can imagine that that stove had something to
do. We were divided into messes and each mess took
its turn at the stove. We got along very well with the
cooking. As for the sleeping, those that had blankets
made a bed of them on the floor. As there were no
blankets in our party, we made our bed on the floor
without blankets.

When we entered this room, the prisoners already
there told us to conceal carefully any money or anything else we had that we didn't want stolen, and to
cut holes in our clothes. We had only been there a few
hours when we found out why we were so advised.

The guards on duty in and around the building were relieved every day at noon. The sergeant and squad of men that came to relieve the guards on duty required all of the prisoners to stand up in rows to be counted. The sergeant counted and the soldiers searched each man in turn. Not only our party that had just arrived but every man in the room, and strange to say, although this searching process had been gone through with by every new guard that had come on duty since the first prisoners were kept there, hardly a day passed but some rebel succeeded in finding something that had been successfully concealed through all previous searches. I remember of a breastpin being found concealed in the hem of a man's woolen shirt after he had been searched daily for weeks. And every day some such new find was made, and, of course, kept by the finder as spoils of war.

The old democratic maxim, " To the victor belongs the spoils," was never more thoroughly practiced than by those same democrats who had charge of that rebel prison.

The search of the new comers was always more thorough than the rest. Our party, being warned, did not furnish much in the way of spoils, though every man who had failed to slit his clothes lost them. Sometimes the reb. would exchange what he had on for what the Yank had and sometimes he would take it without exchange.

The only thing that I had left which seemed to excite the cupidity of the cowardly set was a pair of suspenders. These, one of the Johnnies ordered me to

take off. I refused. We had some words and he
stepped back and cocked his gun. A dozen men spoke
up urging me to give up the suspenders, saying they were
not worth the risk of being shot. I gave them up,
though my own opinion was that the man would
not have shot had I braved it out.

Many ingenious plans were contrived to conceal
valuables. Some took apart the brass buttons on their
coats and neatly put them together again with greenbacks inside.   Others took the heels off from boots or
shoes and hollowed them out so as to hide in them
money, jewelry, etc., but the button and heel racket, as
the boys would say these days, the rebels caught on to,
and one day every brass button was taken from the
room and every heel examined.

Thomas Davidson of our party had $90 in green
backs and kept it through all searches. He kept it
between some dirty pieces of brown paper and whenever the Johnnies began to search, he laid his dirty
brown paper on the floor among other litter and let the
robbers tread on it.

We had not been in this room many days when a
rebel put in an appearance who was to us the type of a
new species.   He was a young fellow, not over twenty,
tall, slim, black hair, black eyes, smooth face, and very
handsome. " Handsome is that handsome does," had
no application to him.   He was a handsome rascal, but
there was a reckless abandon, a good humored deviltry
about his rascality, that compelled a kind of ad-
miration.

When he first entered the room he announced that

he was a prisoner, too, and had come to form the acqaintance of his fellow prisoners.

He was dressed in a neatly-fitting suit of home-spun butternut. Long-tailed frock coat, closely fitting pants, broad brimmed hat, and high heeled calf boots. His small hands and long tapered fingers and small feet betokened a long line of genteelly worthless, if not genteel, ancestry. He wore a belt and two six-shooters of the best pattern, and had spurs on his boots. He was under arrest and awaiting trial, as he told us, for some scrape he had been in where a few negroes had been killed.

On his second visit he complained that he had n't had a gallop for so long that he feared that he would forget how to ride, and wanted to know if some Yank did n't want to play horse. Whether or not anyone volunteered I cannot now remember, but he was soon riding Yanks whether they wanted him to or not. He climbed on their backs and would make them gallop, as he called it, up and down the room, using his spurs the same as he would on a horse.

The guards seemed to be afraid of him and the prisoners were either afraid or deemed it more prudent to submit to his devilment than to have a row.

Carr, however, declared that if he was ever called on to play horse he would pitch the rider through the window. Some one told the rebel what Carr had said, and so he proposed to ride Carr.

"All right," said Carr, "you are welcome to ride me if you can, but do n't blame me if you get hurt. I am an ornery sort of a cuss, anyway, and I do n't know

what kind of an animal I would make if I were turned
into a horse."

Those of us who knew Carr best dreaded the result. We felt that this rebel must be a favorite with
the officers in charge, or they would not permit his
wild capers that had become notorious, and although
we believed Carr could take care of himself notwithstanding the revolvers the rebel wore, we could not tell
what the rebel officers might do if the man should be
hurt. We tried to get the rebel to play some other
game. He would not. He wanted to break in a new
horse.

Carr walked to one end of the room. The rebel
got on, and Carr sure enough started as fast as he could
go for the window at the other end of the room, but
the rebel, having been warned, got off before the window was reached. He began to bluster, but had hardly
time to utter a word before Carr was standing close in
front of him. For a moment those two black-eyed men
glared at each other. Carr spoke no word, but something that the rebel saw in his flashing eyes and pallid
face caused him to turn on his heel and propose some
other game.

One day some new prisoners, " fresh fish," were
brought in. They were from the Marine Brigade—
Germans—at least the two officers, a captain and a lieutenant, were Germans. The captain had on a fine pair
of high-topped, patent leather cavalry boots. He also
had a fine meerschaum pipe, a handsomely trimmed,
well-filled bag of the best tobacco, and some money.

Our rebel tormentor began at once to make love to

THE CAPTAIN OF THE "SEA HORSE CAVALRY" LOSES HIS BOOTS.

this Dutch Captain. He smoked and praised his pipe,
admired his boots and told the captain that he would
stand by him and see that these things were not taken
by the rebel guard. And stand by him he did, for
when the new guard came in and the " fresh fish " stood
up with the rest of us to be counted and robbed, this
rebel rascal led the captain to one side and the guards
did not offer to disobey his commands that they should
let this prisoner alone.

That night we were all awakened by loud swearing
in Dutch brogue and a big racket generally: "Help!
Help! Mein Gott! Mein Gott! Mein Gott in Himmel!!
Help everybodies! Help! Help!" and other such ex-
clamations were coming from the Dutch captain, who
was being dragged around the room by his rebel pro-
tector. The rebel had secured the pipe, tobacco and
money, and was engaged in removing the boots, which
the captain had for safety not taken off when he went
to bed. Our sympathies were, of course, with the captain, but the scene as a sequel to the solicitous friendship of the previous day, and the mixture of Dutch
and Dutch brogue, that poured from the mouth of the
captain, was so comical that we could not restrain our
laughter. The captain always said afterwards that
" Doze Yankee vat makes de big laugh bes a dam site
vurse in my esteem dan der Johnnies vot stole mine
boots."

The next day the rebel brought in a cob pipe for
the captain and allowed him to fill it from the orna-
mental tobacco pouch. The rebel was smoking the
meerschaum pipe, which he said had been presented to

him by one of the officers of the "Sea Horse Cavalry."

These were samples of the capers of that handsome rascal. He was one of a very numerous class well described by Sherman on page 337, of Volume I. of his memoirs, where he says:

"Fourth. The young bloods of the South, sons of planters, lawyers about towns, good billiard players and sportsmen, men who never did do any work and never will. War suits them and the rascals are brave, fine riders, bold to rashness, and dangerous subjects in every sense. They care not a sou for niggers, land, or anything. They hate Yankees per se, and do n't bother their brains about the past, present or future. As long as they have good horses, plenty of forage and an open country, they are happy. This is a larger class than most men suppose, and they are the most dangerous set of men that this war has turned loose upon the world. They are splendid riders, first-rate shots and utterly reckless. * * * * * * They are the best cavalry in the world, but it will tax Mr. Chase's genius for finance to supply them with horses. At present horses cost them nothing, for they take where they find and do n't bother their brains who is to pay for them; the same may be said of the corn fields, which have, as they believe, been cultivated by a good-natured people for their especial benefit. We propose to share with them the free use of the corn fields, planted by willing hands that will never gather the crops."

CHAPTER IX.

The railroads from Canton, east, having been destroyed by Sherman on his Meridian campaign, we were
marched on foot across the country. For rations, we
were given each night a sack of meal and some meat.
Our guards seemed to think we needed nothing to cook
in. We mixed the meal with water in buckets, and
then baked it by our camp-fire, either by filling a husk
from an ear of corn, tying the end and covering it in
the ashes, or by spreading stiff dough on a board and
standing it up before the fire.

After several days of such marching we arrived
footsore and weary at a railroad station, and from there
we were taken on the cars to Selma, Alabama.

The country between the Tombigbee and Alabama
rivers that we crossed on the way, seemed to me then
to be the finest and richest that I had ever seen. From
Selma, we were taken to Cahaba, twelve miles below,
on the Alabama river. Here we joined a still larger
body of Union soldiers who had been taken prisoners.
With our party, there were in all five or six hundred.

The prison was a large cotton warehouse. The
outer wall was of brick and enclosed a large circle. Inside, a circle of posts twenty or thirty feet from the

wall supported the roof which sloped outward to the wall. The circle inside the posts was uncovered. Under a portion of the roof, bunks had been built, one over another, for the prisoners to sleep on. These were more than full before our arrival and we had to take up our quarters on the ground, there being no floor in the enclosure.

We were here two or three weeks, during which time nothing of importance transpired. We thought then that we were most inhumanly treated because we were given no bedding or blankets, and nothing but the ground to sleep on. Otherwise, we had nothing to complain of; our food was wholesome and sufficient.

The two officers in charge of the prison, a captain and a lieutenant, whose names I would gladly mention if I could remember them, were gentlemen. We did not know enough then about life in rebel prisons to fully appreciate their kindness. Every day on the arrival of the mail, one of them would bring in a late paper, stand up on a box and read the news. In many other ways, such as procuring writing material and forwarding letters for us, they manifested such kindly feeling as one honorable soldier will always manifest toward a brother soldier, enemy though he be, in misfortune.

On our arrival at Cahaba, we were taken, a few at a time, into a room, where these officers had each of us thoroughly searched, telling us at the same time to give up everything in the line of knives, jewelry, watches, or money, and that they would keep a list of everything and return all at a proper time. We thought this a

ruse to get us to give up what few things we had managed to secrete from all previous searches. Let it be
said to their honor, that they carried out their promises
to the letter, and that when we were taken from Cahaba
to Andersonville prison-pen, they came in and returned to every Cahaba prisoner the articles taken, as
shown by the list. They then expressed their sorrow
and shame for the horrors of that awful place.

One thing they did which was wrong, if they did it
knowingly. The day we were to leave Cahaba, one of
them came in to read as usual, and read from a paper
a long account of an arrangement having been made
for an exchange of prisoners. They led us to believe
that we were to be taken at once to the place agreed
on for exchange, thus preventing many of us from making an attempt to escape, as we surely would have done,
had we not been deluded by the hope of exchange.

I must not, however, leave Cahaba without mention
of one example of truly chivalrous conduct. Soon
after entering that prison, I noticed that many of the
prisoners were reading books, and pamphlets, histories,
novels, and books on philosophy, science, and religion.
Some of these books were new and nicely bound,
others much worn and evidently the worse for prison
use. By inquiring, I found that these books were furnished to the prisoners by a young lady who lived near
the prison, and that by sending a request by one of the
rebel guards, I could get a book. I accordingly wrote
a polite note, saying that I would be glad to borrow
something to read, and sent it to this lady by one of
the rebel guards. He returned with one of Scott's

novels. Having read this, I returned it and got another, and had something to read all the time I was there, as did every other prisoner who so desired.

The books she sent, whether all her own or borrowed in part, were almost all so badly worn and soiled by the constant use in hands none too clean, as to be of little value afterward. In fact, that young lady sacrificed her library for our sakes; and, in doing so, she furnished the only example that I ever witnessed or of which I have ever heard, of disinterested kindness to a Yankee prisoner from a rebel lady.

The note I sent out for books was addressed to Miss Belle Gardner. Returning the first book obtained, I sent a note of thanks and a request for another book and so on, making each note a little longer and a little less formal until I drew from her a short note in reply. Then with each new book I got a note.

Young as I was, naturally fond of adventure, and the natural bent of my mind stimulated by constant reading of Scott's, Bulwer's and other novels, is it any wonder that my correspondence with this young lady began to seem to me romantic, and that I began to entertain for her feelings stronger than those of gratitude? I was not head over heels in love, badly mashed as you boys of to-day would say, but I was conscious of a turbulent desire to see my kind but unknown correspondent.

There was an enclosure or yard around the door of the prison where we did our washing and cooking. It was a high board fence, the boards nailed on up and down close together. Only those whose turn it was

EAGER FOR A GLIMPSE OF THE DAMSEL.

to do the cooking for a mess were allowed to be in this yard. One day when I was out there as cook, I ascertained from a guard that Miss Belle lived in a house across the street. Then I enlarged the crack between two boards of the fence with a jack-knife, making a hole large enough so that I could get a good view of the house. There was no trouble about getting into this yard; all I had to do was to take the place of some one whose turn it was to cook and who found no pleasure in the task. For several days, most of my time was spent at my hole in the wall, eager for a glimpse of the damsel whom my excited imagination had pictured as possessing all the beauty, loveliness, grace and other heroine qualities of a Rebecca.

My vigils were never rewarded. I sent her a note requesting her to appear at a certain hour on the porch. She never appeared. Then I cultivated the acquaintance of one of the guards, and was in a fair way to arrange through him for a meeting outside the prison, when orders came for our removal, and the conditions and materials for an exquisite romance in real life were rudely broken and scattered.

CHAPTER X.

In the spring of 1884, just after the opening chapter of this little book was written, finding it almost impossible to write with any satisfaction while subject to the usual interruptions and annoyance of business life, I resolved to cut loose from all communications and devote a few weeks exclusively to the work in hand. Besides, I had often thought I would like to see that Southern country again, and that a trip over the old war path would quicken my recollection of the places and incidents about which I wished to write. Of course I visited Cahaba.

I arrived at Selma early in April, just twenty years to a day from the time I went through there a prisoner of war.

Selma is a beautiful city of five or six thousand people, situated on the Alabama river, and in the "black belt" of Alabama. I had always supposed that the "black belt" of Alabama was a region where black negroes were thicker than elsewhere. It is the region of black soil. I was not far out of the way, however, because the negroes are thicker in the "black belt" than elsewhere.

I shall always remember with pleasure my ride on

that delightful April morning from Selma down the river to Cahaba. April there corresponds to June here in South Dakota. I rode horseback. It was to me like riding through a botanical paradise. Spring-time just blooming into summer and such a profusion of flowers. There were great trees loaded with blossoms, and the ground was covered with flowers in full bloom. Where the road passed through cultivated land, the hedge on each side was covered with the Cherokee rose, and was a solid mass of variegated color. There were great, tall pine trees covered to the top with the blossoms of the Cherokee rose. And then the music in the air from the thousands of feathered songsters, each singing as though it were trying to drown the notes of all the rest.

It was Saturday, and market day. The road was thronged with negroes going to market. What subjects there for an artist's sketch-book. All kinds and conditions of the farming class of negroes. Some on foot, carrying bundles on their heads. Some on mules or horses, carrying all manner of truck before and behind; some in carts or wagons drawn by mules or horses, or a horse and a mule, and sometimes a mule and an ox. Old, broken-down horses, lame or blind, or both, hitched to older and worse broken buggies and carriages, with old straps and ropes, which were tied together for harness. Men, women, and children; it seemed as though no member of any family had staid at home. Chickens, ducks, geese, pigs, sheep, a fatted calf, garden truck, butter, eggs, and one bale of cotton, were being hauled, carried or " toted " to market.

One day spent at the market in Selma, on market-day, will give a man a better idea of the condition of the freedmen of the South than he can get by reading all the speeches on that subject that have been printed in the Congressional Globe, during the last twenty years.

I had remembered Cahaba as a bright little town of two or three thousand inhabitants. As I approached the place that morning, I noticed with some surprise that the road instead of becoming better traveled, was dwindling away to a mere wood road, such as the use from an ordinary farm would make. Coming out of the woods to the river bank and looking across to where I expected to see a city, behold there were but a few; and those apparently abandoned, houses. There is an old-fashioned ferry worked with poles. It takes nearly an hour of yelling to bring the ferryman, who explains to me that " De City of Cahaba mos' all been moved to Selma." Cahaba was once the capital of Alabama. Before the war, it was the county seat and a prosperous place; had a railroad; the county seat was moved to Selma, and then the town died. The railroad was abandoned, and most of the brick houses were taken down and transported on boats to Selma and other places. To a Northern man, it seems strange that a town located on a navigable river, with railroad communications could be brought so low.

There was nothing there, not even a brick or stone, nothing but a rank growth of weeds to mark the place where the old prison warehouse stood. Only a few white families were left in the place, and these were

very poor. I found a white man, George Brenner, who
was one of the guards when the Yankee prisoners were
there. He knew the Gardners; was living in the house
that was occupied by them when I was a prisoner. It
was not the house that I had watched so long and so
anxiously through my hole in the fence. I had been
the victim of a guard's mistake. This man told me that
the Gardners were living in Selma.

I was much interested in this "Deserted Village."
It is a charming site for a city, and on the banks of one
of the most beautiful rivers in the world.

About half a mile from the center of the old town,
there stands an old mansion, not old enough to have
shown the ravages of time had there been no years of
neglect, which is, on a smaller scale, almost a fac-simile
of the White House at Washington. It is white,
finished on the outside in imitation of stone, has an im-
posing porch with Grecian columns, grand hall and
stairway, and large rooms with high ceilings. The ex-
tensive grounds are artistically laid out. There are
graveled walks, flowers, shrubbery, and trees in endless
variety. There are two artesian wells, one of them
said to be the second in rank in all the world, measured
by the force with which the water comes out. It was
out of repair when I was there, but the old woman in
charge said that if I were to drop a twenty-dollar gold
piece into the pipe, it would fly right up in the air. I
took her word for it.

All this property is under the charge of one old
negro woman. She had lived there a long time before
the war as a slave, and I sat for hours listening to her

stories of the grand old times she used to see in that
mansion ; weddings, balls, parties that lasted for weeks.
It was one of the places where in her days of wealth
and lavish hospitality, the "Sunny South" had been
wont to gather her "beauty and her chivalry."

What a delightful story it would make if some such
writer as Cable should re-people that old town and that
old mansion, and weave into fiction the facts that such
old negroes could give.

I found Mrs. Amanda Gardner living with her
daughter Belle, in a rented house in Selma. She is over
60 years old, but quite active for one of that age. She
is of good family, and in every sense, a lady of culture
and refinement. She is a fluent talker and uses elegant
language. One of the leading men of the place told me
that Mrs. Gardner had the reputation of being one of
the kindest-hearted and most intelligent women in the
country. The daughter, Belle, is a dressmaker, an
occupation she very much dislikes, but is compelled to
follow, in order to earn a living for herself and mother.
Belle was only a little girl of thirteen or fourteen, in
April, 1864, and wore short dresses.

Mrs. Gardner was during the war, and still is, for
that matter, a thorough rebel. That is, she believed
the South was right, and still believes so. She had one
son killed early in the war, and another, a mere boy,
was in the service and was taken prisoner at Selma, by
General Wilson's cavalry. Wilson's men had heard of
Mrs. Gardner's kindness to Union prisoners, and as a
token of appreciation, they set her boy at liberty and
sent him home to his mother.

Mrs. Gardner said that when the prison was established at Cahaba, she had a large library of choice books that had been given to her by her uncle, Judge Beverly Walker, of Augusta. It was his private library, and he gave it to her when he broke up house-keeping. She said that her heart was moved to pity by the forlorn condition of the prisoners, and she began to loan them books. She had all the standard poets, in handsome binding. Scott's, Dickens', and Lytton's novels, and many others in complete sets. Histories, biographies, books of travel, works on science, philosophy, and religion. A large and well-selected private library. Nearly all of these books were completely worn out. Only those in calf binding and on the less interesting subjects of philosophy, science, and religion, were left whole, and even these were much worn and soiled. I saw in a second-hand store and auction house at Selma, where she had placed them for sale, two or three dozen of those worn and soiled books, all that was left of Mrs. Gardner's once elegant library.

Lending books was not all that Mrs. Gardner did. She took especial interest in those that became sick, and procured and furnished them with suitable food and medicines. Several were nursed in her own house. When winter came, many of the prisoners had no blankets and but little clothing. She gave them everything she had in her house that she could possibly spare, and procured all she could from her neighbors. Said she took up every carpet she had and cut it into pieces the size of a blanket, in order to relieve the sufferings of those poor prisoners.

These things were not done in a corner. Mrs. Gardner was arraigned, either before the church or some citizens' meeting, on the charge of being a Union woman, and of furnishing aid and comfort to the enemy. Captain H. H. N. Henderson, who had the immediate charge of the prison, came to her relief and boldly defended her, endorsing all she had done. Had it not been for his assistance, she would doubtless have been found guilty, and banished. I presume that he is the officer that had charge of the prison when I was there, and who went with us to Andersonville.

Mrs. Gardner showed me over one hundred notes written by prisoners, some addressed to her, and some to Miss Belle. These tell the story of what she did, and at the same time furnish indisputable proof of it. She had two bundles of these notes containing requests and acknowledgments, but she lost one bundle when she moved from Cahaba to Selma. I did not find among those she had, any that were written by myself. She has also received since the war a good many letters from prisoners whom she befriended, and some have remembered her with presents.

When I saw the proofs that Mrs. Gardner possessed of the things she did, and the sacrifices she made for Union prisoners, I supposed it would be the easiest thing in the world to get Congress to pass an act for her relief and remuneration. I at once opened correspondence with senators and members of the House. They all said to pass such an act would be to let down the bars for thousands of other claims in which there was no merit. It would be a precedent that they dare not establish. Something ought to be done for Mrs. Gardner. She is old and poor, and is probably the only southern lady of rebel sentiments, who actuated by Christian charity alone, furnished aid and comfort to distressed Union prisoners.

NOTE.—Mrs. Amanda Gardner is now living with her daughter Belle, in New York. She is at this date, February, 1888, seventy-two years old. Her address is No. 4 West Thirteenth street. The following are samples of the notes she has kept that were sent her by Union prisoners:

MILITARY PRISON, }
CAHABA, ALA., June 4th, }

Mrs. Amanda Gardner: Will you please send some books to the subscribers to while away the hours of prison life.   Respectfully,
J. R. BOWEN,
CHAS. REYNOLDS,
CHAS. HARRIS,
JAMES FARRELL.

CASTLE MORGAN, June 5th.
Mrs. Amanda Gardner: Please accept my thanks for the loan of this; be kind enough to send me another.   CHAS. HARRIS,
Co. K, 13th Ills. Vol.

CAHABA PRISON, March 14th.
Mrs. Gardner: If you please to send me some nice interesting book to read and I will return it with care.   B. F. DAUGHTERY,
Private of Co. 8, 37th Reg't. Ills. Inft. Vol.

PRISON.
Mrs. Gardner: Will you please let five of us have your washing machine and tub to wash some clothes.   CLEMENT BALLINGER.

CAHABA, ALA., March 5, 1865.
Mrs. Amanda Gardner:
KIND MADAM—We are all about to bid farewell to Castle Morgan. Some are already on their homeward journey; we will soon follow, rejoicing we are once more free. I feel I cannot leave without first expressing my heartfelt thanks to you for the noble and humane kindness you have so generously bestowed upon the prisoners while confined here; aiding them by the kind dispensation of your books among them, to while away the tedious hours of captivity both pleasantly and instructively, which otherwise would have been passed in discontent and lonesome weariness. I regret exceedingly, that there were some among them, who were so worthless, as to abuse your books in a shameful manner, but the majority appreciating the noble impulses of thy generous heart, were careful in the use of the works, knowing full well that you were making a noble sacrifice

of your library for their benefit. I regret that one of the books returned to you entitled "Famous Persons and Places," is so badly abused; it was stolen from me and for a long time I knew not what had become of it; after making repeated inquiries it was returned to me in its present condition. Trusting you will pardon me, as I regret exceedingly that such a thing occurred. Be assured, kind Madam, that when we are once more surrounded by kind and loving friends, and in the enjoyment of all that makes life happy and agreeable, our thoughts will often revert to our kind Benefactress at Cahaba; many a silent prayer will be sent heavenward, that you and your lovely family may be spared the horrors of this unnatural and relentless war. Many a man will speak in glowing terms of thy noble generosity, and you will ever be remembered as a friend of the unfortunate. The day is not far distant when Peace the great tranquilizer, will again unite our distracted country in perfect harmony and unity. The end is fast approachi.g when we may again enjoy all the requisites that make life both pleasant and agreeable. *Civil and Religious Liberty* is just as sure to *rule* supreme, as Jehovah guides the Universe.

May Heaven's richest blessings descend upon you and your darling family; and when you are called hence to that " bourne whence no traveler returns," may you ascend to that glorious abode of angels, "where wars, and rumors of wars are never heard," is the wish of one who is happy to subscribe himself your well wisher. Farewell.

Very respectfully,

C. W. HAYES,

Hospital Steward, 3rd. Ills. Vol. Cavalry.

———

CAHABA PRISON.

Mrs. Gardner: Will you please send a book to read. I will take care of it, and return it in good order.   GEO. H. CHADWICK,

Co. C, 1st Ills. Cav.

———

Mrs. Gardner: May the blessing of God ever descend upon thy devoted head, for your kind consideration concerning the unfortunate, is the prayer of one who appreciates the noble impulses of thy generous heart.

Yours in friendship,   A PRISONER.

ADDRESS:
   " *Mrs. Amanda Gardner,*
            Cahaba, Alabama.
   A lady of excellent worth, and a friend to those in distress."

———

CAHABA, ALA., PRISON, }
April 11, 1864. }

Mrs. Gardner: Please lend me " Botta's History." I will take good care of it and return when done. Your Ob't Serv't,   JAS. B. SLUSSER,

3rd Ills. Cav. Vol.

———

CASTLE MORGAN, }
July 8, '64. }

Mrs. A. Gardner:

DEAR MADAM—I return the book that you lent me, and am very much obliged to you for it. I have taken the best care of it that I could. If you have the other volume of the same work, I would be very glad if you would lend it to me; and if not, I am glad to get any book that is interesting.

Yours Respectfully,

WILLIAM ENGLISH,

Co. F, 7th Ky. Cav.

CAHABA, ALA.,
July 11th, 1864.

Madam: In returning the accompanying books with many thanks, I would respectfully beg of you the loan of another, Yours obediently,

J. W. S. BEATTIE,
2d La. Fed. Cavalry.

Madam: Will you be so kind as to send me—a prisoner—one or two books to pass away the time. Having heard from our men how kind you have been in sending reading matter to them, I make so bold in addressing you in my behalf. I have the honor to be, very respectfully, your obedient servant,

THOS MCELROY,
To—   Capt. U. S. Navy.
Mrs. Gardner.

CAHABA PRISON, May 21st.

Mrs. Gardner: Please excuse me for troubling you for a little vinegar, as I have a high fever every day and crave it and I believe it would do me much good.   Yours with respect,   MICHAEL O'FARREL,
118th Ill. Mt'd. Inft.

APRIL 15th, 1864.

Will Mrs. Gardner please send me a book to read, and oblige,
Very Resp't,   JAMES MILLER,
4th U.S. Cav.

CAHABA, Jan. 18th, 1864.

Respected Madam: An unfortunate prisoner of war begs you will excuse the liberty he has taken in thus addressing you. Your many acts of kindness to us will ever be gratefully remembered. If possible to repay you, how gladly would we. But Madam we know your noble heart would resent any such offering, and we have only the opportunity left us of returning you the heartfelt thanks of all the prisoners. And now I trespass on your kindness still further. My time for service has nearly expired. I do most earnestly desire to be exchanged. If within your power, by your kindly influence, to assist me, the remembrance of the happiness you would confer on an unfortunate man, I am sure, would amply repay your generous nature.

I am, most respectfully,
ANDREW MCFARLAND.

NOTE—My mother secured his exchange, and he went his way rejoicing.
—BELLE GARDNER.

CHAPTER XI.

I have already stated that we were moved from Cahaba to Andersonville. Before starting, three days' rations of meat, rice and meal were issued to us. Unfortunately, we cooked it all, and before we reached Montgomery, by steamboat — it is needless to remark that we were all deck passengers—our rations of rice and meal had soured, and could not be eaten. At Montgomery, the officers procured all the meal they could for us, but not enough to go round. There we were put on flat-cars, some in box-cars, and started, as we were told, to Savannah to be exchanged.

At Columbus, our locomotive gave out and our rations likewise, and we stopped for repairs. We were there from noon of one day until afternoon of the next. Although we were all without food and hungry, and made our necessities known to hundreds of people that flocked around to see us, an ear of corn each was all we received. I was satisfied that the officers in charge tried to do better by us, but there was no quartermaster there, and they had no money with which to pay for what the citizens were unwilling to give. We heard many such remarks as: " Let the damn Yankees starve. They will soon learn to do without eating and they may as well begin now, etc." Had we known then what we soon after learned, we would surely have made a break for liberty.

There was an old unoccupied hotel building near the railroad track, and our guards allowed some of us to go into it to pass the night. It was a beautiful moon-light-evening, and a crowd of young people, boys and young ladies, gathered there to see us. Some of our boys began to sing Union songs. Then the Southern girls gave us a rebel song, and directly we were having a song-battle, and turn about, we fired songs at each other until long into the night.

At Fort Valley, in Georgia, we were turned on to a track that we knew did not lead to Savannah, and by inquiring from those who came around to see the Yan-kee prisoners, we learned that Andersonville, the great prison-pen, was on the road ahead of us. Our guards, too, were doubled there. But though our hopes of im-mediate exchange began to vanish, little did we dream what Andersonville meant. We supposed it to be some-thing like Cahaba, and though that was not a comfort-able place, it was endurable. We were out of food when we got to Columbus. Forty-eight hours after-ward, we came in sight of a stockade in which, we were told, there were 20,000 Union soldiers. Forty-eight hours without other food than a little corn, makes a healthy man hungry. I was not only healthy, but young and growing. I was hungry, but I thought to myself, in fact it was the expressed thought of all, we will soon be among friends who will be glad to re-lieve our pressing wants. In this instance, there was more pleasure in anticipation than in participation.

No pen, no words can describe, no pencil can approach the scene that burst upon our astonished eyes, as we entered the gate of that—I shall not call it infernal, nor terrible, nor horrible, nor hell's hole, but simply Andersonville; and hereafter when a writer would describe a misery so infernal, or depict a horror so atrocious that no suitable words can be found in any language, let him merely liken it unto the miseries and horrors of Andersonville.

The sun was just setting when we started from the station to the prison. It was about dark when we reached the outer gate. As we approached, sounds came to our ears, at first like the roaring of the sea, heard a long way off. Drawing nearer, the noise resembled somewhat that made by a large army going into camp. It was unlike the noise of an army or the roar of a large city, because there were no sounds of wheels or rattle of tools. It was a Babel of human voices only. There was something strangely doleful and ominous, even in those sounds.

The gates were thrown open. On each side of what seemed a street, leaving room for us to pass in column of twos, we saw a dense mass of beings. Those in the front ranks held in their hands cups, cans and little pails, and chunks of bread. They are there, we thought, to hand us food as we pass. We entered. The line on either side was a line of living, human skeletons, walking mummies ; ragged, many nearly naked, all skin and bone, black as Indians, not exactly smoked Yanks, but the smoked skeletons of Yanks.

WE ENTER ANDERSONVILLE.

We were hungry. These men seemed to be starved. There they stood, their great eyes protruding beyond their gaunt and bony cheeks; their limbs, half covered, showed great swollen joints, black, bruised-looking elbows and knees, and great puff-balls for feet. The feet of many, looked like boxing gloves. All this we saw in sections, as it were, by the uncanny, flickering smoking light of a pine knot torch or a " fat" pine stick, that here and there one of the creatures held in his hand.

> "The brows of (these) men, by the despairing light,
> Wore an unearthly aspect, as by fits
> The flashes fell upon them."

Yes, nearly every one of the front rank had food or wood in his hands, but not to give. They were there to barter or to sell. The majority of us had nothing with which to buy, nothing to trade. We did not ask for anything. There was that in these surroundings which, if it did not make us forget our hunger, made us feel that our misery was not worthy of mention. I have noticed that beggars on a street do not solicit alms while a funeral procession is going by.

We stood a long time in that street before we were assigned even a portion of bare ground on which to stretch our weary limbs. The two rebel officers who had been in charge of us from Cahaba, set about getting us something to eat. About 10 o'clock, rations were sent in; a pint of corn meal and a little salt for each man. Raw meal and salt! How cook it? What in? What with? In all that pen, you couldn't pick up enough wood to make a match. We had nothing to draw our rations in, much less to cook them in. I turned the sleeve of my jacket, tied the end with a piece of the lining, and in this, received a quart of meal for myself and Lynn B. Cook. We were bunk-mates or bed-fellows, without either bunk or bed. Some mixed their meal and salt with a little water and ate it raw. Others bought or traded for a little wood and borrowed pans in which to bake. Cook and myself found a Grant county man from a Wisconsin regiment, who was kind enough to lend us a skillet and a little wood. Our hunger appeased, we lay down on the bare ground without cover or shelter, to sleep, and thus we passed our first night in Andersonville.

The next morning we were counted off into divisions, ninety in a divison. Twelve divisions formed what was called a detachment. To each detachment was allotted a small piece of bare ground on which to camp. We were told that this bare ground to sleep on, a scant pint of meal, a quarter of a pound of meat or its equivalent in rice or beans, and a piece of green wood as large as a small piece of stove wood, these once each day, and a spoonfull of salt once each week, were what we would get, and all we would get to live on.

Are we to have no tents, no blankets, nothing to cook in? No! Will we not be given, or allowed to get, forks and poles and brush with which to make a shelter that will protect us from the scorching sun and the pitiless rain? No! You have your ground, you will get your rations, nothing more. Is it surprising that we could hardly believe our ears, that stout hearts quailed, and strong men lost their courage and lay down broken in spirit?

Andersonville is situated in the sparsely settled piney woods of southern Georgia. It is a rolling country abounding in creeks and swamps. Pine trees cover the high land, and along the streams and swamps there are gum and other trees that flourish in wet soil, and thick underbrush.

The prison was made by enclosing sixteen acres of this land by a stockade. The stockade was made of logs twenty-five feet long, uniform in size, hewed on two sides, set upright and close together in a ditch five feet deep. The dirt being filled in and tamped around the bottom, these logs form a solid wooden wall twenty-five feet above the ground. On the outside of this wall, at regular intervals of about sixty yards, scaffolds were built with steps leading up to them, and on these scaffolds, which were three feet lower than the top of the wall, the guards stood.

On the inside of this wall and twenty-five feet from it, is the dead-line. This is a row of posts driven into the ground with poles or narrow boards nailed on top so as to form a railing three feet high all around the inside of the stockade.

This sixteen-acre pen or field, was a rectangle in form, the east and west sides longer than the north and south. A small stream ran through from west to east dividing the interior into what was called north and south sides. This stream furnished the water supply and the sewerage. The sink was at the lower end of the stream. Forks driven into the grounds supported poles upon which the prisoners sat, their droppings falling into the stream. Above the sink, the stream was used for washing and bathing. Water for cooking and drinking was obtained between the little bridge that crosses the stream and the dead-line on the west side. The ground on each side of this stream is a gently sloping hillside. Adjoining the creek on the north side there is about two acres of wet, boggy, miry, swamp.

The entrances to the prison, two huge gates, are on the west side. One on each side of the creek and midway between creek and corner of stockade. There is a small stockade yard around each gate on the outside. When prisoners are brought in, or the wagons loaded with rations, they pass through an outer gate into this yard, the outer gate is then barred before the gates to the main stockade is opened. This to prevent prisoners making a sudden rush for an open gate. The fastenings to these gates are on the outside. Leading across the prison from each gate there is a street wide enough to turn a wagon in. There are two or three other streets of considerable width. Leave out the creek and the two acres of swamp, the broader streets and the twenty-foot strip between the dead-line and the stockade, in all at least four acres, and you have left twelve acres for the prisoners to camp on, to cook, eat, and sleep on. There were 20,000 prisoners there when we entered. Twenty thousand on twelve acres. Sixteen hundred and sixty-six on one acre. Ten to each square rod. For each man not quite four by seven feet. Before that stockade was enlarged, there were at least 30,000 prisoners inside of it, crowded on to those twelve acres. Less than three by six feet for each man, just enough for all to lie down on at once, not enough to

have buried them all; giving to each a separate grave.
In July, the stockade was enlarged. About six acres
more of ground were taken in on the north side. Eight
acres in all, about six available for use. The prisoners
increased until there were 45,000. They were as thick
then as before. The following table copied from
McElroy's story of Southern Prisons, is a part of the
report made by Surgeon Joseph Jones, who was sent by
the Surgeon-General of the Confederate army to
examine Andersonville:

Month and Year.	Average number of Federal prisoners	Area of Stockade in square feet.	Average number of square ft. allowed to each prisoner.
March, 1864..........................	7,500	740,520	98.7
April, 1864.........	10,000	740,520	74.0
May, 1864............................	15,000	740,520	49 3
June, 1864...........................	22,291	740,520	33.2
July, 1864...........................	29,030	1,176,120	40.5
August, 1864........................	32,899	1,176,120	35.7

He gives the number of acres as seventeen at first,
and twenty-seven afterward. He makes no deductions
for dead-line, streets, or swamp, and he gives what he
calls the "mean strength of prisoners." The size of
the pen was as I have stated, also the number of
prisoners there. There could be no mistake on these
points because the prison was measured by different
men, and the prisoners were counted daily. But take
the rebel figures and you have less than five by seven
feet for each man in June, and but a fraction over in
August.

CHAPTER XII.

The prisoners who were first turned into Andersonville in February, 1864, were from Belle Isle. These
found the ground covered with underbrush, stumps and
limbs of trees that had been used in making the stockade, and trees that were not large enough to make
stockade logs. It was comparatively easy for these
men to provide themselves with shelter. Some built
huts two or three feet high on the sides with gable roof;
others made dug-outs, by digging cellars and putting
roofs over. The roofs were all made of brush woven
together with a thatching of pine leaves on the outside.
Others made neat little houses by bending poles so that
both ends would stick in the ground; forming a frame
like that of a cover to an emigrant wagon. These
frames were thatched over the sides and top and one
end. Those who came later, when wood and brush
were not so plentiful, had two forks, a pole and blankets
or pieces of tent-cloth stretched over, and thousands,
who came as the Cahaba prisoners did, long after every
limb and stump and pine leaf had either been consumed
or had an owner, had no shelter whatever. These marked
out their six by seven feet, for two, by ditching around
it and raising the surface so that the wash from higher
ground would not flow over it; and there most of them
died. But few of the Cahaba prisoners had blankets,

fewer had anything in the shape of cooking utensils. Neither my bunk-mate, Cook, nor myself had anything except the ragged clothes we wore.

On the first morning, it was the second day of May, the sun rose scorching hot. I went to the tent of the boy who had loaned us the skillet, and asked to borrow a cup so that I could go and get some water. I said to him, " How are we to live? What are we to do, who have no shelter?" " Live! Do!" said he, " Why, all you have to do is to answer at roll-call, draw your rations, and fight lice. If you want to live, do n't go near the dead-line." I soon found out that he had summed up the daily life of the average prisoner in Andersonville.

With the borrowed cup I went for water. We had been warned to keep away from the dead-line. To cross it—it even to get hand, or foot, or head, a hair's breadth over—was instant death. The watchful guards, with unerring aim sent a bullet through every prisoner who by accident or otherwise trespassed on this line. They gave no warning, and I never knew of a shot being fired that did not kill a man. It was said that a thirty days' furlough was the reward for killing a prisoner at the dead-line. To get clean water for drinking or cooking, it was necessary to go near the dead-line where the stream came in. Many men were shot for merely reaching under the dead-line to get a canteen or cup of clean water. On that first morning, I stood within a few feet of one who was filling his can safely inside of the dead-line, when some others, struggling for a place to get water, accidentally pushed him so that he fell with his head under the pole. That instant his brains and blood went floating down the stream and another rebel guard received the coveted furlough.

Another time, I saw some starving men with long willow or cane poles, standing by the dead-line trying to kill for food, swallows that had built their mud nests in the cracks of the stockade, and in the twilight were skimming back and forth as swallows will. One poor, lean, hungry boy knocked a swallow down and reached a fraction too far in his effort to secure it. His spirit went home to Him who watches the sparrows when they fall, and another son of chivalry went home on a furlough. Such scenes were common. These shocked me more than others because I stood near by.

SHOT AT THE DEAD LINE.

CHAPTER XIII.

For thirty successive nights after we entered this pen, it rained hard every night. The days were scorching hot. The rain soaked us at night. The sun blistered by day. The nights were cold—at least they seemed cold. Food is the fuel that warms the body. We had not sufficient food, and, therefore, we were colder at night than well-fed men would have been. The cold made us hungry, and hunger in turn made us cold.

Very few men were turned into Andersonville who lived very long without in some way securing more than the common ration to eat. For the first two or three weeks I lived, or rather slowly starved on the common ration. I weighed about 160 pounds when I entered the place. A few weeks after, my thumb and finger would meet around the largest part of my arm over the shirt and jacket sleeves. Every day while suf- fering from hunger, I would resolve and re-resolve that when I got my ration, I would divide it into three parts, be they ever so small, and eat at morning, noon and night. I never could do it. Every time the ration came, I devoured it all, and all was not enough.

The wood that was issued with the rations, was obtained by letting a few men from each detachment go to the woods under guard and bring in what they could carry on their backs. One man was allowed to go each day from each division of ninety. What he could carry in was divided so much to each mess of ten. The cooking was done by messes, and the food when cooked was carefully divided into as many little piles as there were hungry men in the mess. Then one man would turn his back, and another pointing to a ration would say, "Who shall have this?" The man whose back was turned, sometimes he was blind-folded also, would call a name. As each man's name was called, he would step up and take his share. It always seemed to me that the smallest pile in the lot fell to me.

Going out after wood was a coveted task. Only the strongest were chosen to go. When a prisoner could manage to get out with those who were selected to carry wood without being specially detailed from any division, it was called "flanking out."

The flanker kept for himself all that he could carry in. Lynn and myself soon learned the flanking game, and we soon managed to get enough pine boughs and limbs of trees to build quite a little house. Thomas Davidson, who had succeeded in eluding all searchers and carried into Andersonville $80 or $90 in greenbacks, joined Lynn and myself in making our shelter. When we had it finished and nicely thatched all over with pine boughs, and more pine boughs to sleep on, and a wide blanket which Davidson bought, to sleep under at night, we were living in the lap of luxury, as compared with

those who were compelled to lie at night on the bare
ground in the pelting rain, shivering and aching with the
cold, and to endure without shade or shelter the scorching sun at noon-day.

We had been there but two or three weeks when,
instead of raw meal and meat, our rations were brought
in cooked. Then there was no more flanking out, be-'
cause there was no further use, that is no absolute necessity for wood. Those who were brought in after that
without money or blankets, fared even worse than we,
for there was no way for them to get any shelter.
Neither must it be understood that many of the Cahaba
prisoners were as fortunate as myself and Cook.

The cooked rations were worse in many respects
than the raw. When our meal and meat, or sometimes
beans and molasses, or rice in place of the meat, came
to us raw, we could cook it in various ways. We could
make a stew with meal dumplings, or a soup of the
beans. Or we could make bread or cakes of the meal,
as we saw fit. Out of so little variety in food, skillful
cooking could make many different dishes. When the
cooked rations came, they were always the same. The
meal was cooked in large pans for bread, or boiled into
mush, and the meat always boiled. At the cook-house,
usually strong bacon, sometimes beef, was put into great
cauldrons and boiled. No pains were taken to clean it;
then to save salt, the filthy slop from which the meat
was taken, was used in mixing the meal. The meal was
coarse and not sifted. When this cooking was done,
the great, square loaves of corn-bread (they were about
two by four feet, and four inches thick) were piled on

wagons, the meat piled on the bread, and hauled into the prison. The beef brought in was always more or less tainted. The bacon was always strong. When mush was made and brought in in barrels, it was often sour. The result of eating this coarse bread, bran and all, and the greasy meat, was first to bring on diarrhœa. Weakened by this, the stomach soon became nauseated and refused the food. When the food made a man sick, and being sick, he could not eat the only food there was, starvation began.

Thousands taken in this way lived but a few weeks. Those who recovered from the diarrhœa had next to battle with the scurvy. The scurvy could neither be prevented nor cured without vegetables, such as onions and potatoes, cabbages and melons. These, however, could only be had for money, and at a high price. And in this was the worst part of this awful life; men were starving, actually dying by hundreds every day for want of food, and all day long resounded in their ears the cries of hucksters vending their goods from stands, such as you will see at country fairs.

"Walk up, gentlemen! Walk up, and get your nice, warm dinner! Roast meat and potatoes, wheat bread and pure coffee! Walk up, gentlemen! Walk up, and get your nice, warm dinner! Here's your cool lemonade, made right here in the shade, and the best thing in the world for scurvy! Right this way, gentlemen, for your hot chicken soup! Bean soup! Bean soup! Bean soup, only five cents a dish! Bean soup! Bean soup! Ham and eggs! Ham and eggs! Right this way for your ham and eggs with johnny-cake, and huckleberry

pie for desert! Right this way, and get your choice dinner for a dollar!"

The larger huckster stands were located on the
three or four principal streets of the prison, but smaller
stands and peddlers could be seen everywhere, and no
starving prisoner, though he had the will power to keep
his eyes from feasting on what his stomach craved, but
his hands dared not touch, could keep the peddler's cry
and the huckster's call from sounding in his ears all day
long, and far into the night.

Why, you ask, were not these poor, starving prisoners, relieved by those who had this provision to sell?
Why are there out of prisons everywhere, and especially in all great cities, the poor, the hungry, and the
ragged, the sick, the lame and the blind, who are passed
daily without relief, and without compassion by fellow-
men rolling in wealth and debauched by luxury? Andersonville was a world condensed with the forms and
restraints of society left out.

Let a ship sink in sight of the shore and a hundred
helpless men who cannot swim be thrown into the sea
—ten of them seize planks that will keep them from
sinking. Does any man give his plank to one of the
ninety who is about to go down? The prisoner turned
into Andersonville with nothing, and depending wholly
on his keepers for support, was as helpless and almost
as sure to perish as the wrecked man without a plank
in the sea. A blanket to cover him, a few boughs, out
of which to form a shelter, a few dollars to dole out
sparingly for daily wants, were to him as precious as the
life-preserver is to the wrecked mariner at sea.

Friends worked together and helped each other. Old comrades formed into messes and in a measure made common store, but the general rule was, every man for himself.

There were men there well-dressed, even to dandyism, who sported watch and chain, had rolls of money and spent dollars at a meal. These could have given, but did not, just as millionaires who have more than they can ever possibly consume, think only of gain, and seldom give and grudgingly, to the struggling poor. Begging was almost as rare as giving. The poor fellows seemed to realize that as a rule, to part with even a morsel of food was to lessen their chances for life. Tobacco was not considered one of the necessaries, and to ask a chew or pipe of tobacco was not considered begging, and when asked was seldom refused by those who had it in sight.

Probably half the prisoners had resources other than the daily ration. There were hucksters, and peddlers, bakers, tailors, even jewelers, gamblers of every kind, chuck-luck, faro, poker, wheel of fortune, tricks and games of every variety were played and carried on openly and publicly. The rattle of dice, the whirring of wheels, and the cries to attract the crowd, chimed in with the huckster's call and peddler's cry to make the din and racket of the streets. All of these men thus engaged had something besides the daily ration.

During the first few weeks, these things were not so extensively carried on. The prisoners who first entered Andersonville were from Belle Islane and other prisons, and were poor, but from the time I got there, there were almost daily accessions of prisoners, fresh from the battle fields around Richmond, and from the armies of the west. These, especially those from around Richmond, were not searched and robbed as we had been, and as most prisoners taken from the west were. They came in, as we used to say, with flying colors, bringing blankets, knapsacks, canteens, and cooking utensils, money and jewelry.

A brigade, several regiments and a battery, in all about 3,000 men, taken at Plymouth, N. C., had received their veteran bounty and new clothes, with which to go home on veteran furlough, but a few days before their capture. They were taken on conditional surrender, and one of the conditions was, that private property was to be respected. They came in about the middle of May, with their entire camp outfit, tents and all, and must have had an average of hundreds of dollars in money to the man. Previous to their arrival, hucksters handled but small stocks of tobacco, meal, beans, rice, potatoes, wood, etc., and the peddler's cry usually was, " Who wants to trade rice for beans!" or, " a pone of bread for a dish of soup!" or, " a ration of meat for a ration of meal!" and the gambling was all on a small scale. Soon after the arrival of the Plymouth prisoners, bedlam was indeed let loose. Peddlers and hucksters multiplied, gamblers and tricksters increased, and new kinds of business sprung up.

The hucksters obtained supplies, in part from the prison suttler, who had a store in the prison under the protection of the rebels in command, and in part from those of the prisoners who went outside to carry out the sick to the hospital, or the dead to the dead-house, and who managed to carry on trade with the rebels on the outside, and smuggle in goods. The officers, too, who came in once a day, one or two to each division, to call the roll of the prisoners, were nearly all smugglers, and brought in tobacco, eggs, and other articles that they could conceal about their person, to trade and sell to the prisoners.

The profits in smuggled goods were so much greater than on those bought at wholesale from the prison suttler, that a separate branch of trade sprung up, which was selling chances to go outside. For instance, a sick man would go, or get his friends to carry him out to sick-call. If, on being examined by the rebel physician, he was ticketed for the hospital, and, if he could not walk, as was usually the case, there would be a chance for two other prisoners to go under guard and carry the sick man on a stretcher to the hospital. This chance to go out belonged to the companions who had assisted him to sick-call. They would often sell it to others engaged in the smuggling business, and the smuggler buying such a chance, would often realize a handsome profit on goods that he could buy on the outside of the guards and other traders, and bring in concealed in his clothes, or in the pine boughs, or a hollow log, which he would be allowed to carry in.

In this way, the dead soon became articles of merchandise, and were bought and sold. The number that died in camp daily, especially in July and August, was from 50 to 120, according to the state of the weather.

DEAD YANKEE'S BECOME ARTICLES OF MERCHANDISE.

After a stormy day and night, there would be many
more dead than during the same number of hours
of fair weather. The dead were carried' to the
gate every morning, and laid in a line commencing at
the dead-line and reaching back into the prison.
Each corpse was carried to the dead-house on a
stretcher by two prisoners guarded by a rebel soldier.
The corpse of a prisoner belonged to his bed-fellow,
if he had one, if not, to his mess-mates, who had the
disposal of the chances (two of them) to go with the
stretcher to the dead-house. Smugglers bought these
chances, also.

The first man brought to the dead-line in the morning, would be taken out first, and they would be taken
two or three at a time, according to the number of
guards detailed. The first smugglers out in the morning would have the best chance to trade, and so the
chance to carry out the first corpse was worth more,
and sold for more, than the chance to go out with one
that would not be reached until later. It soon became
the custom for the price of a corpse to be written on a
piece of paper and pinned to the rags of the corpse.
The first dozen or so, would be marked as high, sometimes, as three dollars each, and if there were eighty or
a hundred, in the row of corpses, as low as fifty cents
would buy some of the last. If you paid three dollars
for a corpse, you would get out early while trade was
brisk, and before the best bargains were gone. If you
paid fifty cents for a corpse, you had to sit by it perhaps
until afternoon, and watch it to keep it from being
stolen, and when it did come your turn to go, the stench

of your corpse would make you sick, and chances for trade would be slim.

I saw many fights over the disputed ownership of dead bodies. I remember one in particular. A poor, starved creature who seemed to have no friend, had for a long time been in the habit of coming at night and lying down just outside of my shanty, close up to the side where I slept. When he thus lay down, there would be nothing between us but a thin thatching of pine leaves. He was literally alive with vermin, and would no sooner lay down than I would be awakened by the lice crawling over my face, and would get up and drag the poor fellow away, sometimes twice in one night. One morning after I had thus dragged him away, I saw a bloody fight going on between two men, and going to the spot, found that they were fighting because each claimed to be the next friend, and, therefore, the owner of the body of the man who had died where I had left him. I often heard it said that death was sometimes assisted by the would-be mourners, that the corpse might reach the dead-line among the first in the morning.

Great God! Think of it. Men brought so low by the thousand, systematically and purposely too, and by their own countrymen, civilized, christianized, chivalrous countrymen, that to save life, to get food and wood, where food and wood were plenty, they will barter and sell, and fight over the dead bodies of their friends. What are Heathen?

I bought a chance once to go out with a dead body. I had to carry the end of a stretcher on which the head

lay, because the man at the other end had been hungry
so much that he was thin and weak. The stretcher was
an old gunny-sack nailed to poles. The sack part was
too short. The feet hung over it at one end and the
head at mine. There had been no tender, loving hand,
to close those eyes when the last breath had gone.
They were open wide and glaring. The head hung over
the end of the stretcher and the eyes glared up at me.
They haunted me for weeks. I never bought another
corpse.

Aside from the sickening stench of that corpse, and
the ghostly glaring of those open eyes, how unspeakably
delightful were the moments I spent that morning out
of the prison. You enter a conservatory or garden full
of freshly blossomed flowers, and the odors are delicious,
but you cannot discern the perfume of the green grass,
and common plants, and trees of the hills and fields
around you, because they are in your daily air. Neither
can you detect the obnoxious odors of a room which
you entered when the air was pure, and stayed in until
it was foul. So I did not know how foul the stench of
the prison was until I went out that morning and tasted
fresh air. The bark of the trees, the leaves, the grass,
the decaying wood, the flowers, each had a distinct and
easily-distinguished odor. The common air was frag-
rant. I drank in great draughts of it as though it were
a new, delicious and exhilarating beverage, and so it
was. But when I re-entered the pen, the foulness there
was just as noticeable as the fragrance outside had been,
and I was sorry that I had gone at all.

Besides the traders and peddlers who earned money

with which to buy extra rations, and those who brought money in, there were others who received extra rations. For instance, there was a Yankee sergeant or quartermaster for each detachment who received the provision each day for his detachment and divided it into as many parts as there were divisions in a detachment. He received three extra rations. Then the sergeant of each division who received from the detachment sergeant and distributed to the sergeant of messes, received two extra rations, and mess sergeants, some of them, received one. Whether these extra rations were issued in addition to the rations for the common prisoners or whether they were taken from and diminished the daily supply for the prison, I cannot say. My opinion was that the latter was the fact.

Others received extra rations by repeating. At roll-call each detachment formed in line, and a rebel sergeant, accompanied usually by one or two guards, came in to call the roll. They called the roll of one division of ninety at a time, and then counted the men in line to see that the number tallied with the roll; then passed to the next division, the whole detachment being required to stand in line until the roll of all the divisions was called. Suppose a man from the 1st division died during the night, some man from some other division of the detachment would slip into the vacant place, stand there and answer to the dead man's name, and as soon as that division was counted, slip back to his place and be ready to answer to his own name in his own division. As there were as many rations issued each   day   as   there   were   prisoners   at   roll-call   each morning, the repeater would get an extra ration.

The rebels knew that something of the kind was going on, and they tried many schemes to prevent it, but never wholly succeeded. Probably one-half of the prisoners at Andersonville, especially between June 1st and September 1st, of 1864, in one way or another of the several ways mentioned, secured more to eat than was provided for and issued to them by the authorities. Of this half, a large percentage lived, for Andersonville was naturally a healthy place. Of the other one-half who had no extra rations, no aid of any kind, and many no shelter, nearly the whole died.

I have never met a survivor of Andersonville, whose daily ration of food during the whole, or at least, the most of the time he was there, was not in some way supplemented, and I very much doubt whether there is now a man living who endured five months of 1864 in Andersonville, with nothing to live on save what the rebels furnished.

CHAPTER XIV.

The horrors of Andersonville did not result entirely from the prison system and management planned
and authorized by the rebel authorities and their agents.
It is even doubtful which furnished the most extreme
cases of human cruelty and depravity, the rebels, or the
prisoners themselves. When we first entered the place,
we were cautioned to look out for raiders. These
were at first a small band of roughs from New York
City, who had been engaged previous to their capture,
in what was called bounty jumping. They were called
"bounty jumpers." Large bounties, or sums of money
wer, offered by the state to those who would enlist, and
sometimes, a man who was drafted would pay a large
sum to some other man to go as his substitute. These
fellows, it was said, had been engaged in enlisting for
these state and private bounties, remaining in the service long enough to get the money, and then taking the
first opportunity to desert and go back and enlist again
in some other place, under another name, and secure
another bounty. They were confined at first at Belle
Island, and there banded together to steal and rob, and
there received the name of raiders. As the number of
prisoners who had anything for robbers to take, increased, the raiders also grew in numbers and boldness.
The accessions to the gang, were probably not all

bounty jumpers. At first, their operations were after the sneak-thief order. A haversack, or a blanket, or clothing would be snatched at night from some sleeping prisoners. The thief would run and soon be out of sight among the huts and tents, and pals of the raiders would put any pursuer off the track. Becoming bolder, they began to work in parties of five or six armed with clubs, and they would enter at night the sleeping place or tent of the victim marked in the daytime, and forcibly take whatever suited their fancy, mercilessly clubbing, sometimes killing any unfortunate man who dared resist. And so they went from bad to worse. The Ninetys' organized to defend each other against the raiders, and then the raiders banded together and strengthened their forces. If a party of raiders, or an individual raider made an attempt to rob that led to the alarm of a Ninety, and could not escape with the plunder, a shrill blast from the whistle which each carried would bring others to the rescue; a bloody fight with knives and clubs would ensue, and almost always the raiders would be victorious, for they were a well-fed band of strong, desperate men, practiced and skilled in such warfare, and were under leaders whom they obeyed. A few such men attacking suddenly in the night could usually get away with their plunder before the surprised friends of the parties being robbed could gather in sufficient numbers to successfully resist.

After the Plymouth prisoners came in, and money became plenty, the raiders became high-toned and did not stop to meddle with anything of less value than watches, jewelry and money. They carried things with a high hand; the men engaged in trade, and others known to have money, were their chosen victims. The leaders even grew so bold as to go around in broad daylight and demand of the leading hucksters money, in return for which they would grant the hucksters exemption from a raid for so long a time. Those who would not pay were spotted, as it was called, and soon paid a visit that left them penniless, and served as an example to terrify the rest.

It soon became evident that murders were being committed. Men who had money or other valuables, would disappear, and their friends having no reason to believe they had made their escape, could find no trace of them. Suspicion pointed to the raiders, but there was no proof. Finally the raids became so common, the levying of blackmail so frequent and notorious, and so many men were missed whom it was supposed were murdered, that the whole prison began to be aroused, and the question of a general organization to establish rules and put down the raiders, was frequently discussed. There seemed to be no one who dared to lead off in such a movement. The belief was universal that any man who dared to take the initiative, would be spotted and surely murdered by the raiders. Finally the raiders themselves aroused the very man who, of all others there, was best calculated to lead in breaking their power. This man was known as "Limber Jim."

Limber Jim was one of the Cahaba prisoners. He was a tall, slim, wiry man, good looking, good hearted, full of energy, a lover of fun, and was at Cahaba, as at Andersonville, the best known and most popular man in the prison. He had, it was said, traveled with a circus before the war, and it is very likely that as clown or actor in a circus he acquired not only his nickname, Limber Jim, but also the inexhaustible fund of anecdote and glibness of tongue that enabled him to be so entertaining and rendered him so well known and popular. Soon after we entered Andersonville, "Limber," as we called him for short, invented "root beer." He obtained in some way a large barrel, filled it with water, sorghum, molasses, and corn meal. This mixture soon worked and acquired a sourish, sharp taste, similar to, but not nearly so pleasant, as the taste of the old-fashioned metheglin, made of honey and water.

The sassafras tree abounds in that portion of Georgia, and Limber had obtained, by digging them from the ground in the prison, a lot of sassafras roots. These he boiled, and with the tea, flavored his beer, and called it "root beer." Mounted on his beer barrel, or on a box, Limber would draw a crowd by telling jokes or stories, or by singing a song, and then he would expatiate on the health-giving, disease-curing properties of his "root beer." It was, according to his talk, a panacea for all the ills that prison life was heir to. It was good for scurvy, and that was the disease that scourged us most. When the Plymouth men came in, Limber got rich. He sold hundreds of barrels at 5 cents a glass that cost less than that many cents per gallon. Then he went into trade generally, and besides beer kept everything to sell that could be obtained. I have heard that he won money at poker, and ran a faro bank with great success. I did not see him do either.

I do know that he acquired a large amount of money—several thousand dollars. He secured for his mess a large tent that would hold twelve or fifteen men, pitched it on the South side, where the raiders were mostly congregated, had all of his mess-mates armed with knives and clubs, and had two of the largest and strongest men of the whole prison employed to stand guard over this tent at night. Here Limber and his guards and friends lived like kings.

At first the raiders let Limber alone, probably because he was such a favorite and had so many friends. Afterward they were kept off by his giant guards.

One evening, however, Limber went down to the creek alone, and three of the boldest of the raiders saw him. This was the opportunity that they long had sought, but a sad day for them was the day they tackled Limber Jim. One big burly Irishman caught him from behind, put an arm around his neck, under his chin, drew him back and held him nearly choked, while the others searched his clothes.

The day after the robbery of Limber Jim a plan for an organization was agreed upon by the leading men throughout the prison. The rebel authorities were consulted and persuaded to co-operate. A thousand picked men, called regulators, were got together, duly officered, armed with clubs and drilled, and war on the raiders was openly and formally declared. A police justice was elected and police headquarters established. Notice was given throughout the camp, inviting every prisoner who could identify and furnish proof against a raider to report at police headquarters. The

well-known and leading raiders were at once arrested
by the regulators, Limber Jim acting as commander,
and taken outside and there held in irons under strong
guard.   When all that could be identified were thus
taken out, a jury of the sergeants of the detachments
was selected to hear and take testimony against them.
Six of them were, by this jury, indicted for murder in
the first degree, and the bodies of the murdered victims were found buried deep in the ground, under the
tents of the leading raiders.   These six were duly tried
by a jury impaneled for the purpose.   They were con-
fronted with the witnesses against them, permitted to
bring witnesses in their defense, and allowed the benefit of counsel.   In fact, they were granted every right
and privilege guaranteed to a citizen of the United
States by the constitution.   They were all found guilty
by the jury, before whom they were charged, and were
duly sentenced to be hung.

For all the rest who were found guilty of crimes of
lesser degrees than murder, for robbery, theft and the
like, there seemed to be no better mode of punishment,
so they were sentenced to "run the gauntlet."   That is,
all the prisoners who had been robbed, or clubbed, or
raided, or otherwise maltreated by the raiders, were
permitted to form a line on each side of the street leading into the prison from the gate.   The raiders were
turned into the prison, one at a time, and to pass
between these two lines of men, standing there, waiting
for revenge, was "to run the gauntlet."

Had the use of clubs been allowed no raider could
have gone through alive.   Blows and kicks were

unmercifully administered, and many barely escaped
with life. As a rule, those who had been guilty of
the most and the worst crimes received the hardest
drubbing, for, first one and then another of the men in
line would make his charge, stating what the raider
had done, and those against whom the most charges
were made fared the worst.

When the time came for the execution of the six
men convicted of murder, a regular scaffold was
erected inside the prison. It was reported that the
raiders had re-organized, and would make desperate
effort to rescue their leaders and companions at the
scaffold, when they were brought in to be hung. Great
precautions were taken to prevent the success of any
such attempt, should it be made.

The hour came. The thousand regulators were
formed in a hollow square. The six doomed raiders,
hand-cuffed and shackled, were marched in between a
strong guard of rebel soldiers. They were conducted
into the space left near the scaffold, and there turned
over to the hangmen, Limber Jim being chief hangman,
and then the guards went out, for the rebel authorities
had decided to permit, but not to take any part in the
execution of these raiders. The convicts were all
Catholics, and at their request a priest was there to
administer the sacrament, and perform the last rites
of their religion.

The hand-cuffs and shackles are removed and the
six doomed men kneel with their priest to pray. All is
still as death, for death is hovering over the scene.
Suddenly one of them stands on his feet, and giving

the shrill, rallying cry of the raiders, with a spring like
that of a tiger on its prey, he leaps right into the teeth
of the regulators, seizes a club, and in less time than I
can tell it, clears the whole solid mass of regulators,
and leaps and bounds away through the camp.

What a scene! The whole 30,000 prisoners are
looking on, thousands crowded close around the
regulators, and when that raider breaks away every
looker-on supposes that the dreaded raiders have made
the threatened attempt to rescue, and every one starts
at once to get away from the desperate struggle that
is expected to follow. The result is, that the backward
movement takes the crowd like a great wave, and they
tumble over tents, into holes, off from buckets, boxes
and whatever could be secured to stand on, tramping
on each other, yelling, cursing, and fighting, as they
go. It was a terrible panic, and many were sorely
bruised, and some had arms, some legs broken in their
falls.

In the meantime the fleeing raider is hotly pursued.
He dashes into tents, and out by lifting up the edge,
dodges around shanties, and tries in vain to elude the
sleuth-hounds on his track. He is caught! A mass of
regulators gather around and form a hollow square, in
the center of which, struggling still, he is carried back.
There is no more waiting for religious ceremony.
Again, all is still. The raiders beg and plead for mercy.
Their hands are pinioned behind them, the black cowls
drawn over their heads, and they are led each by a
hangman up the steps, on to the scaffold. There,
standing in a row, the loops pass over their heads, the

hangman's knots are adjusted, and the hangmen step down. Limber Jim seizes an ax, drives out the wedge that supports the drop, and five of the murderers are dangling in the air.

The sixth, the same big burly Irishman that mugged Limber Jim, proved too heavy for his rope, and as it broke, he fell through the scaffold to the ground, stunned and bruised, but not killed. Water is dashed into his face and he revives and pleads for mercy. "Surely, yiz have not the heart to hang a man twice," he is heard to say.

With awful coolness, Limber Jim lifts him up, assists him back up the steps of the scaffold, and there, standing on the outer beam, adjusts the noose of the new rope, lifts the man up off his feet and drops him to writhe, and struggle, and twitch, beside his writhing, struggling, twitching companions, until all are dead, dead, dead!

The raiders raided no more. From this time on there was a police commissioner, or justice, and regularly organized police, and all prisoners charged with stealing or violating any of the prison rules were, if convicted, severely punished. Sometimes they were sentenced to do fatigue duty, such as cleaning streets, etc., but the usual punishment was to stretch the offender over a barrel, and whip him on the bare back with a cat-o'-nine tails, the number of lashes given him being in proportion to the grade of the crime. A sanitary organization was also perfected to take in charge the general condition of the prison, see to the cleaning of streets, compel the deposit of urine and excrement at the sink, and enforce personal cleanliness.

The prisoners employed on the police and sanitary forces each received extra rations; subordinates one, officers two, or more, according to the grade of office. Whether these extra rations were taken out of the daily supply for the prison, thus diminishing the quantity issued to the common herd, or whether they were furnished in addition to the daily allowance for the camp, I cannot now say, though it would be interesting to know. One thing is certain. The fact that all service rendered was paid for in extra rations was of itself proof that the common ration was not sufficient. Otherwise who would have labored for an extra ration? I verily believe that a man of, or about the average size, and of ordinary habit as to consumption of food, could not have lived three months with nothing to eat besides the common ration.

CHAPTER XV.

Escape was almost impossible. A few succeeded
in getting away, but in nearly every instance they were
brought back. A pack of blood-hounds was kept, and
every day, or oftener, a squad of cavalry accompanied
by these dogs, would make a circle around the prison a
half mile or more away, and the hounds were so trained
that they would take the track and go in pursuit of any
prisoner who had succeeded in passing the circle. Those
captured were often terribly bitten and mangled by the
dogs, and were subjected to tortures upon their return
—such as hanging by the thumbs, sitting in the stocks,
and working on the chain-gang. Hanging by the
thumbs was to be stretched up by a rope fastened
around each thumb until no weight remained on the
ground, the toes being allowed to merely touch to prevent the body swinging around which would cause sickness and vomiting. The cries of the poor fellows subjected to these tortures were pitiful. They prayed and
begged to be shot. Suppose you were to be taken to a
wooden wall, seated on the ground, your feet made to
project through two holes as high up as they would
reach, and your hands through two other holes higher
up, and your feet and hands thus placed securely fastened, you would be in the stocks.

In the chain-gang, one ankle of each man was fastened by an iron shackle and chained to an immense cannon-ball, perhaps a forty-pounder. When the gang moved from place to place to and from their work, or to the sink as often as any member had to go, each member had to drag a separate ball with one leg and help to drag the large one with the other. Thus shackled, they ate, slept, and worked. Every man who attempted to escape had to pass in turn through these three forms of torture.

I tried many plans for escape. In fact, there was not a day from the time I was made prisoner that I was not looking for a chance to get away, or working out some scheme. I helped to dig one tunnel. We begun it in a hut located near the deadline. Carried the dirt away in sacks at night and put it in the creek. The man who worked at the end of the tunnel lay on his belly or back and dug into the tough, hard red clay until he had loosened a small sack full. He would then pass the sack to a man behind him who would pass it to another, and so on back. When the sack reached the top of the ground, men lying on the ground for the purpose, shoved it from one to another, until it was far enough from the over-looking guard for a man to walk away with it and not be noticed. Progress was slow on account of the extreme hardness of the clay, but we toiled on night after night until we had a tunnel far outside of the stockade. We were waiting for a night dark enough to enable us to make an opening on the outside and get out unseen, when our tunnel shared the fate of

most tunnels that were tried. Some poor famishing
creature, who had seen us at work, in the hope of getting an extra ration as a reward, betrayed us, and in
came an officer and took out all that were found in the
tunnel, or in the tent from which it started, and put
them through the tortures prepared for those who
attempted to escape. Luckily, I was not at the tunnel
at the time.

Few tunnels were successfully completed, because
it was hardly possible, when men were so crowded together, to carry them on without many not engaged in
the work finding it out, and as it was known that old
Wirz would reward the informer, there was always some
poor devil, either naturally mean enough, or so distracted by want and misery, that for the sake of the
reward he would prove traitor to his friends.

One night there was a tremendous rain-storm, and
the water in the creek rose so high that it washed out
several feet of stockade at the lower side. Had this
been generally known a general break would have been
made, but only a few of those quartered near by knew
of it, and some of them escaped by swimming out in
the flood. The rebels soon discovered the break, and
had an armed force around the place on the outside.

This incident suggested to some of us the possibility
of making an organized effort to liberate the entire
body of prisoners. As before stated, the stockade was
made of logs, set close together, the lower ends about
five feet in the ground. Seeing the place where the
washout occurred, suggested the idea of tunneling to
the stockade, and then excavating the dirt from the in-

side, down to, and partly under the bottom of the logs, and for several feet along the camp side, leaving only enough of the top earth to held itself up and conceal the work. The clay, being hard and tough nearly to the surface made this possible. We planned to remove the earth in this way from at least twelve or fifteen feet of the front of the stockade, and we had long poles prepared, intending when all was ready, to put the poles against the top of the stockade logs, and push them over. The dirt all being removed from in front of the logs at the bottom, this was a perfectly practical scheme.

While the excavating was going on we organized a body of picked men; had officers chosen for each company and regiment, and a general and aids. In short, we organized a small army of the strongest and most resolute men. Our intention was to make a sudden rally, surprise and capture all the guards, arm a party of men with the captured guns, and let them make a forced march to Americus, only twelve miles away, and capture the arms and munitions of war stored in the arsenal there. With these we could arm and equip every able-bodied man in the prison. We had planned also to cut the telegraph wires, and to take prisoner every man, woman and child in the neighborhood. Also, to send a small body of men out, who were to provide themselves with horses and arms as they went, and force their way to Sherman's army with all possible speed. These men were to go in a body, if possible, and if not, scatter, and each man go it alone. Some, we thought would surely get through, for Sherman was

then at home in Georgia. The main body of the prisoners, with the arms secured at Americus, were to
march on to Macon, and liberate the officers who were
in prison there, if possible. If the officers were liberated
further movements were to be guided by them. If they
were moved before our forces could surround the place
there, we would take the town and fortify ourselves in
it and hold every inhabitant of the place, and all we
could find and bring in, as hostages, so that if a rebel
army, large enough to overpower us, should come, we
would hold them at bay until succor from Sherman
should arrive, by putting their own people in front of
us, and compelling our enemies to kill their own friends
or let us alone.

It was a well-laid scheme, and it might have succeeded had not a Benedict Arnold sprung up at the
proper time to betray it for reward. One fine morning
we were awakened by the sound of cannon, and the
whistling of grape and canister close over our heads; at
the same time the entire force of guards were seen
forming on commanding portions around the prison.
Then a company of rebels marched in and went to the
exact spot where we had excavated; destroyed our
works, and posted notices, stating that the plot in all its
details was known and that the first sign of any unusual
movement of prisoners would be the signal for firing
the cannon that were trained on the camp and loaded
with grape and canister. At the same time the rebels,
to prevent another attempt of the same kind, fastened
timbers across the logs of the stockade near the top,
and put strong braces against the timbers, so that the

whole stockade was firmly held in place, and could not be pushed over from the inside, even though the dirt was removed from the front.

We never knew to a certainty who the traitor was that betrayed this scheme, but suspicion fastened on a man who had but one leg, and walked with crutches. He was about that time, granted a parole of honor and permitted to pass out and into the prison as he pleased. One day he came inside and a lot of prisoners gathered around him and charged him with having been the traitor. He stoutly denied it, but the prisoners continuing to abuse and threaten him, he attempted to go outside. There was, at the time, no officer at the gate to let him out, and he stepped into the space between the dead-line and the gate, saying to the guard above the gate, that he would stand there until an officer came. The guard told him to go back inside of the dead-line. The poor cripple, standing there on one foot and one crutch, replied, and correctly, too: "You know I have a parole to stay outside when I choose, and there can be no harm in my standing here until an officer comes to let me out; besides those men threaten to kill me, and I am afraid to stay inside the dead-line."

The guard cocked his gun and ordered him to move back inside the stockade. Looking the guard full in the face, the man replied: "I do n't care how soon I die, shoot, if you like!" The words were hardly spoken, when the guard fired. The ball passed through the man's mustache and out through the neck, breaking the bone. Poor fellow, he felt no pain, and another rebel soldier was furloughed for honorable conduct. God

save the mark! All the regulations and commands in
Christendom could not compel a brave and honorable
man to shoot another, a poor cripple, under such circumstances.

There was a hospital at Andersonville to which
sick men were admitted, and where they ought to have
received at least good treatment and care, for the hospital stewards were paroled prisoners, and they certainly ought to, and probably did do the best they could
for their suffering comrades.   But the capacity of the
hospital was limited, and only those, it was said, who
were past curing were taken out.   In fact, so few of
those who were taken there ever came back, that it
came to be the prevailing idea that to go to the hospital
was to be carried alive to your grave, and but few sick
prisoners, unless taken by force would go there.   There
was a sick-call too every morning at which time the sick
could go into a smaller pen just outside the south gate
where a number of rebel surgeons prescribed for the
sick. The prevailing complaints were scurvy, diarrhœa,
and malarial and other fevers. A little vinegar and
sulphur was doled out to the scurvy patients; what the
rest received, I do not know. I do know that I had
the scurvy bad and that the stuff I got at sick-call did
me no good, but that when I got money and bought and
ate a few raw potatoes and some other wholesome
food, I was quickly cured.

There was at one time, a small-pox scare. Whether
there were cases in the prison, I do not now remember.
At any rate, the rebel physicians received orders to vac-
cinate every prisoner who could not show a fresh scar.

We were formed in line, and those who could not show
a fresh scar were vaccinated whether they wanted to be
or not.   I had been vaccinated a year before and
escaped.   Hundreds died or lost their arms from the
effect of the vaccine.   Some said it was poison, or dis-
eased matter purposely used.   I do not think so, but I
do think that many of the prisoners who had the scurvy
and other blood disorders, were not in fit condition to
be vaccinated; that because of their condition the sores
made became inflamed, gangrene got into them and
proved fatal.   I do n't think small-pox could have made
any head-way among the half-starved prisoners; they
were too lean.

CHAPTER XVI.

The miseries of Andersonville during the rainy months of May and June for those who had little or no shelter, who, drenched by the cold pelting rain, shivered all night, and had to endure the blistering intolerable heat of a tropical sun by day, were indescribable. How shall I convey to you an idea of the increased suffering in July and August, when the rains, which before washed the camp and carried off the filth, ceased; when there were more men to the square rod, when the rations were poorer in kind and less in quantity, when the creek that furnished water had diminished in volume and had been polluted by all manner of filth from the camps of the guards and the prison cook-houses above; when the accommodations at the sink were not sufficient for half of the prisoners, and, more than all, when hunger, and exposure, and disease, and scurvy, and gangrene, and vermin, and noxious vapors, and despondency had worked together for months and left their awful marks upon so many thousands of helpless men? The mind naturally shrinks from the appalling task. Abler pens than mine have been engaged upon the subject. Books have been written and many letters published describing the horrors of Andersonville, and yet the half has never, and never

can, be told. I can add, as it were, but a mite, and all
I shall seek to do will be to leave in the mind of the
reader a picture of the place such as memory brings
to mine.

I give below a table copied from "McElroy's
Andersonville," compiled from the official reports
made by confederate authorities. It gives the average
number of prisoners during the months of July and
August at a little less than 32,000. My own recollection, and it is supported by that of many others, is that
there were between 35,000 and 40,000, and that the
death rate was correspondingly larger. It is quite
likely we were prone to exaggerate—just possible that
a rebel officer would under-rate.

*The number of prisoners in the Stockade, the number of deaths each month,
and the daily average, is given as follows:*

MONTHS.	NUMBER IN STOCKADE	DEATHS.	DAILY AV'R'GE
March	4,703	283	9
April	9,577	592	19
May..	18,454	711	23
June	26,367	1,202	40
*July..	31,678	1,742	56
August	31,633	3,076	99
September	8,218	2,790	90
October..	4,208	1,595	51
November	1,359	485	10

    * In July one in every eighteen died.
      In August one in every eleven died.

The greatest number of deaths is reported to have occurred on August 23,
when 127 died, or one man every eleven minutes. The greatest number of
prisoners in the stockade is stated to have been August 8, when there were 33,114.

What were all these men doing? Not reading,
for there was no Mrs. Gardner with a humane heart
and willing hand in that vicinity. There were no
books there except a few testaments and bibles. In

my opinion the first thing that would attract the notice
of a stranger was the thousands of men sitting in the
sun, nearly naked, picking away at their clothes—
picking off the lice. The place was literally alive with
lice and fleas. Every man who did not get so sick and
weak and discouraged that he had to lie down and be
eaten up by them, made it one of his daily tasks to take
off all his clothes and pick off the lice and fleas. To
do this effectually, you must hold the garment in the
warm sun so that the vermin would crawl out and be
seen. So through all the hottest part of the day, there
were thousands and thousands of men sitting on the
ground wholly or partially naked picking vermin from
their old rags or clothes, if they still had them; thousands were nearly naked when they had all their clothes
on, these were all more or less afflicted with the scurvy.

Scurvy swells the gums, and in time, rots them so
that the teeth fall out; the feet swell and puff up especially if the man is bare-footed, until they are two great
puff-balls, resembling a pair of boxing gloves. Grasp
one of these puffed feet with your hand, and your fingers will make dents in the flesh that will but slowly fill
out, as in a piece of rising dough. The knee joints, too,
are favorite points for scurvy. They were always
swollen, like the feet, but black and blue, as though
they had been pounded into one horrible bruise.

Now, picture one of these half-naked, bony, filthy,
gaunt and ghastly skeletons, his eyes sunken, his cheek
bones protruding, his gums all swollen, his elbows and
knees swollen, and black and blue, and his feet two
great shapeless masses of bloated flesh, and picture him

sitting on the ground, as he usually was, with his chin between his knees, and his hands clasped around them, and you have a specimen of "Smoked Yank," thousands of whom could always be seen at a glance.

I have mentioned the swamp. I shrink from the task, but I must take you there. The privy, or sink, as it was called for the prison, was, as before stated, two lines of poles supported by forks, one line on each side of the creek. As the prison filled up, and the accommodations at the sink became insufficient, the swampy ground had to be used, until, finally, that whole piece of swamp ground was covered with one connected mass of human excrement. A moving, seething mass, for vermin, worms, and bugs, kept it moving. Now, take the specimen of "Smoked Yank," as I have described him. Let him drag his swollen feet along one of the paths left to walk in, through that seething, squirming mass, and then, when he finds a place to stoop, his swollen knees refuse support, he falls over; is too weak to get up or crawl out, and there he dies. Yes, such scenes were there, and too common. There were hundreds of such cases. Would no one help him? you say. Certainly, if asked, or if the dying man was noticed. But when men became so weak and low, they were liable to fall over in a swoon, and not be noticed, especially at night. I have helped carry men out, who had fallen over in that way, and did not call for help. They seemed to think their strength would return, and enable them to get up.

I remember having my attention called one day by most terrible oaths, coming from a man who lay on the side hill, just out of the swamp. I went close to him. He seemed to be delirious. He lay there with maggots and worms crawling in and out of his ears and his nose; lice all over him; flies buzzing around; maggots and worms between his fingers and his toes. And there he lay, seemingly without strength to move, and from his mouth there poured the most fearful stream of oaths I ever heard. It seemed that he blamed President Lincoln for not arranging an exchange, and on his head the burden of the oaths fell. He also cursed the Union, cursed the confederacy, and cursed God for permitting his condition. He lay in that condition, cursing and moaning, for several days before he died. And scenes like that were not uncommon; there were hundreds, barring the oaths. True, such deaths were not the rule, for usually, the sick and helpless were faithfully and tenderly cared for by their friends and companions, even until death. Those whose friends had all died, or who had become partly, or wholly, demented, and got in the habit of wandering around alone, were the ones that furnished such examples of extreme horrible misery.

There are in the National Cemetery at Andersonville 14,000 grave-stones.

I was in Andersonville from the 2d day of May until about the 1st of October, 1864. During that time about 12,000 of the prisoners died, an average of eighty for each day. The direct cause of this terrible death rate was the crowding of so many into so small a space, without sufficient food and shelter. A larger prison, and more and better food it was in the power of the

confederacy to furnish. As for shelter, the pine forest
that surrounded the prison for miles in every direction,
would have furnished shelter and beds in abundance,
had the prisoners been allowed to go under guard, or
on parole, and help themselves. For the confederates
who had control of rebel prisons there is absolutely no
excuse. They were murderers, cool, calculating, merci-
less workers of a worse instrument of torture and death
than the bloody days of the French guillotine, and gib-
bet, and stretching-rack, ever furnished. And those in
authority at Washington, at the time, from Lincoln
down are not blameless. The rebels claimed that they
were always willing and anxious to exchange prisoners,
but that an exchange could not be agreed on, because
our authorities would not enter into any agreement
that did not recognize the freed negroes, who had enlisted in the Union army as soldiers, and entitled to be
exchanged, the same as white men.

As a matter of pure principle, this was probably
correct, but as a matter of public policy, and of justice
and mercy to the white Union soldiers, who had enlisted
before there were any freed negroes, it was all wrong.
If there had been any considerable number of negro
soldiers in the prison suffering with the others, there
would then have been a vital principle of justice, as well
as honor at stake, and the white prisoners themselves
would have been the last men in the world to have
sacrificed that principle in order to secure their own
liberty and lives. There was not a negro Union soldier
in Andersonville, or in any other prison for any considerable time. When they were captured they were

either sent back to their old masters, or put to work on rebel fortifications. And they were not starved, and did not suffer. They were property in the eyes of the confederates, and as such were taken care of. Their condition as prisoners was little worse than it had always been before the war. Stanton, and others who insisted on that point, might as well have insisted that every black in the South, whose liberty had been granted him by the Emancipation Proclamation, and who was detained by his old master, should be a subject of exchange.

I do not know who was responsible for that fearful blunder, but a blunder it was, and every prisoner knew and felt it to be such. The men who stood out and refused to exchange, unless the negroes were recognized by the rebels as Union soldiers, and exchanged with the rest, did it too, knowingly and advisedly. The prison authorities once permitted the prisoners to send to Washington three of their number, chosen for that purpose, who took with them a petition to the President, asking that an immediate exchange be agreed to, on the terms proposed by the rebels, and setting out fully and plainly the suffering that was being endured, and the loss of life daily occurring. This petition was signed by thousands, and is probably now on file among the records of the war. Nothing came of it. There was a political principle, a cold, naked, clean-cut principle, at stake. There are many thousand grave-stones at Andersonville which would not be there, and many thousand widows and orphans in the land who would not have been widows and orphans so

soon, but for the mistaken zeal and cold-blooded principles of those in authority at that time.

When it was all over, and thousands of the poor
emaciated creatures that survived were sent home,
and scattered through the land, and the truth became
known, and Harper's Weekly, and other illustrated
papers, sent out pictures of the starved heroes, then a
storm of indignation arose which threatened to burst
over the heads of the misguided statesmen, who had ·
refused to exchange. Then something must be done;
Andersonville must be avenged; the storm must be
averted. And something was done; Andersonville was
avenged; poor old Wirz was hung. Poor old Wirz—a
miserable, excitable little foreigner; a cross, I always
thought, of Dutch, Italian, and French, with nothing
Dutch about him, except his pipe and his brogue;
nothing French except his nervous excitability; and
nothing Italian, except his low cunning. Wirz was n't
a man of anywhere near the average ability of our
private soldiers. He only wore a number six hat. He
sometimes came into the prison, and some prisoner, to
annoy him, would sing out: "Sour crout." Wirz
would draw his revolver and run in the direction of the
voice. Then some one behind would yell: "Go it,
Dutchie." Failing to find the first man, he would run
after the second, and so on. I have seen him charging
around in that way, like an escaped lunatic, swearing in
Dutch brogue, for half an hour at a time. It fitly illus-
trates the calibre of the man. Think of such a man,
and he only a captain in rank, being hung to avenge
Andersonville.

' Wirz had charge of the prison as a kind of provost marshal. He received and issued the rations, and faithfully executed his orders. But as to his being in any manner to blame for the lack of food and shelter, and for the smallness of the pen, and such other evils, I don't believe he had anything to do with it. General Winder was the commissary-general of rebel prisons. He established the prison and knew all about it. I saw him there with his staff, twice myself. Wirz was only one of his subordinates, and he was probably only a tool of somebody higher than himself in authority.

I don't suppose Wirz would have been hung had not specific acts of wanton cruelty to prisoners, not justified by the prison rules, been proved against him. God knows he deserved hanging bad enough, but as there were thousands of men against whom specific acts of cruelty, and of murder, during the war, could have been proved, who were not tried, I take it that Wirz was really hung to attract the attention of the people, and keep some of the blame from falling where it belonged. I read the account of his trial at the time, and it was my opinion then, that to hang Wirz and let Davis, and all others who were over him, go free, was a cowardly piece of business on the part of our government.

Had a few prominent men, generals and congressmen, been starved to death in Andersonville, Davis, and all others in authority would have been hung. Abraham Lincoln was painlessly, artistically removed. Booth, who performed the act, was killed, and all those who could in any way be connected with the planning of it, four in all, were hung, and justly, too. Thousands of soldiers were removed at Andersonville, and the work was not painlessly nor artistically done. Wirz, a half-witted foreigner, was hung. Lincoln was president; the Andersonville victims were all privates. This is a republic!

CHAPTER XVII.

Fortunes have been made by exhibiting panoramic pictures of Gettysburg, Shiloh, Sedan, and other noted battle-fields; why not exhibit Andersonville? The loss of life was greater than at any battle of the war. More men were killed there than were lost in the Vicksburg campaign, including the many that died from sickness. There are as many grave-stones at Andersonville as are in the National Cemetery at Vicksburg, where the Union dead are collected from all the battle-fields and camp-grounds in that vicinity. A fortune awaits the man who shows Andersonville in any large city as those battle-fields have been shown. Greater than fortune, renown, compared to which that of Munkacsy will be nothing, awaits the artist who will do justice to Andersonville on canvas.

Ambitious painter, come. Bring your brush and your easel. Fill in with details true to life these outlines, and fortune and fame are yours!

Two side-hills with a creek running between. That's right. Now, the swamp ground on the north side. There you have it. Now, the stockade and the dead-line. Guards leaning over the top of the stockade with a longing-to-go-home on furlough look in their eyes, as they eagerly watch the dead-line. Have you got the eyes? All right; touch them up later. The gates next, and the streets—that's so, if the shanties and hovels·

are put in, the streets will be left. I can't help you
much on the shanties. Every conceivable form of shelter from sun and rain that Yankee ingenuity could contrive and make out of logs, limbs, brush, poles, blankets,
pine leaves for thatching; some had tents and sun-dried
bricks. Give your fancy play; you will hardly invent
one that could not have been found there. Oh, yes,
there are photographs; did n't think of them, they will
help you out. How close together shall you put them?
Well, give the rebels the benefit of the doubt, if there
is any; allow four by six feet to each man, but out of
that you must save room to pass between the rows of
hovels. Now, we must have on each side of these
streets, booths and board counters on which hucksters
have for sale goods and provisions, meats, bread, pies,
cakes, potatoes, onions, cabbage, and fruit. To use a
couplet from Barbara Frietchie, with a little change,
makes them look,—

> " Fair as a garden of the Lord,
> To the eyes of the famished Union horde."

Under tents and sheds fronting on these streets,
tasty lunch-counters, and well equipped restaurants with
waiters in attendance. Tobacco and cigar stands,
chuck-a-luck and faro boards, wheel-of-fortune, and
gambling tents with men sitting at cards. On a corner
near the center, the sutler's depot containing flour in
bags, tobacco in boxes, every variety of sutler goods in
wholesale quantities. Standing in front of all these
boards, counters and stands, rows of able-bodied and
well-dressed men, eating, smoking, gambling, spending
money as freely and as gaily as at a Northern fair.

Behind them, a pack of moving skeletons in rags, grimy and black from smoke, feasting their eyes, ready to grab up and fight for any crust of bread, or bone, or melon rind, or stub of cigar that might be cast among them. Often I have seen men buy food, and to see the fun as they called it, cast it among this hungry, ragged rabble, and watch them scramble for it and often fight over it. Men would buy watermelon by the slice, eat the meat and throw the rind on the ground to see it snatched up and ravenously devoured. The rinds and seeds of melons were eagerly sought for as cures for scurvy.

We must have here and there an oven built of clay, where pies and bread are baked; barber shops, tailor shops, jewelry shops, with lettered signs on all these. Thousands of naked men sitting where the sun could shine on their clothes, picking off lice. Thousands more lying on the ground and in the hovels in the delirium of fever, or dying from hunger and the ravages of scurvy; kind comrades leaning over to bathe parched lips and fevered brows, and whisper to them of the far off home, to rouse their failing courage.

And now the sink with its crowded poles and crowds standing by watching, struggling for a place, the creek above full of men bathing and lined by others washing clothes, and above them, where the water came in under the dead-line, a crowd with buckets formed in lines and taking each his turn as it comes to dip his can or bucket or cup and get clean water. Now and then one reaches too far or is pushed from behind across the fatal line, and his brains and blood float down among the bathers.

Now, put in the skeletons with poles striking at the skimming swallows. A hundred corpses laid in a row at the south gate all nearly naked, on the breast of each a slip of paper and a price, and sitting at the head of each one an owner watching either to sell his corpse or for his turn to carry it out.

Near the same gate, show the poor one-legged man on his crutch and the fire from the gun of the guard above, reaching clear to his face, as it did.

Now cover the swamp with its seething, squirming mass of corruption, with here and there a helpless being lying in it. Show a hundred more scattered around under the scorching sun in the last stages of scurvy, with flies, and maggots, and lice feeding upon them, and groans and curses ;—no, you cannot paint groans and curses. You cannot paint the din and racket and roar. It was not enough that thousands should die from disease brought on by hunger and exposure, and made fatal by lack of medicine and care—they must die with the food and vegetables that would save their lives, in sight. With the peddler's cry and the huckster's call, offering for sale dainty dishes, sounding all day in their ears. These things you cannot paint no more than you can the feelings they caused in the minds of starving men.

CHAPTER XVIII.

HOW I MANAGE TO LIVE — MY BUNK-MATE GOES TO THE HOSPITAL. — I SECURE A CORNER LOT, AND GET INTO TRADE—SHERMAN'S FINE-TOOTH COMBS AND SCISSORS —REMOVAL TO FLORENCE, SOUTH CAROLINA.

I now come to what will be of more interest, at least to my boys. They want to know how I managed to live where so many died. As before stated, my bunk-mate, Cook, and myself, went into the Andersonville prison penniless and entirely destitute in every way. The clothes we had on had been cut into holes, to keep them from being taken when we were at Canton, Miss. We began, at first, to flank out with those detailed to bring in wood. In this way we secured our part of a shanty, made of brush and boughs. We sold some of the wood that we secured flanking out. A little bundle of "fat" pine, as much as a common stove stick would make, when split up fine, brought twenty-five cents in the prison. Such bundles of "fat" pine are now sold in southern cities, especially at Atlanta, Georgia, where I lately saw them, for one cent. They are used for kindling. We used them to boil our little cans of mush. One little blaze held under a can would keep it boiling, and a small bundle of the wood lasted a prisoner several days. You could light one end of a piece of good "fat" pine," stick the other end in the ground, and it would burn there like a candle. The smoke from that kind of wood is something like a mixture of soot and oil. It made us all black. It took good soap and warm water to make any impression on it. Water could be warmed in the sun, but soap was scarce. With the money we got for wood, Lynn and I managed to piece out our rations so as to live.

We had only been there two or three weeks, when we began to get cooked rations. After that there was no more flanking out. The coarse corn bread made Lynn sick. It soon became so loathsome to him that he could not eat it at all. In that condition a man could die of hunger with piles of the corn bread in his bed. In spite of all I could do for Lynn he grew gradually worse. I walked for hours, trying to trade his corn bread and strong meat for beans or rice, or something that he could eat. Often I could not, because too many wanted to trade the same way.

Davidson, our partner in the shanty, had money. I persuaded him to loan me ten dollars. With this money I started a small huckster stand. Sold salt, rice, beans, tobacco, and such things as I could manage with so little capital. Prices were so high that you could put in one pocket ten dollars' worth of such articles. With the profits from this stand I got for Lynn a little food which he could eat. Before I had gained enough to make a start of my own, the raiders became so bad that Davidson was afraid I would get robbed. I had to pay him back and quit. Then Lynn thought he would try the hospital. We had not yet learned that but very few who went there recovered. We carried him to sick-call. He was admitted to the hospital. Within a few weeks we learned that he was dead. No braver boy   or   better   comrade   ever   wore   the   blue.

After Lynn went to the hospital, I put in a few weeks digging tunnels and trying to find a chance or contrive a plan for escape. During these weeks I had nothing to eat but my rations, I got so thin that there was nothing of me but skin and bone. The scurvy got hold of me, my gums swelled and my teeth got sore and loose ; my knees were swollen and my feet puffed and bloated. I began to realise that I must get help or die, and I suffered from hunger. Had I lost my grip then I would have been a goner. The harder the lines were drawn the more was I determined to live it out.

About this time the prison was enlarged by taking in eight acres adjoining the old stockade on the north. Certain detachments were designated to occupy this new ground, which was covered with the boughs and limbs of the trees that had been cut down for the new stockade. My detachment was not one that was to go, but I managed to flank in and to secure a footing, and build a shanty on the main street of the new part and at a good place for trade. As soon as the ground in the new part was divided off and occupied, the old stockade between the old and the new parts was turned over to the prisoners, and a general scramble for the stockade logs began. I took part in that with some success.

I now had a shanty on one of the best places in the prison for a huckster's stand. How I managed to hold it I cannot now remember. I was a squatter, pure and simple, with no right whatever to ground, even to sleep on, in that part of the prison, but hold it I did.

Limber Jim was one of the Cahaba prisoners. He had got rich selling his famous "root beer" and running a big stand. I showed him my fine location and asked him to start me in business. He did so ; in fact, he said he wanted to go out of the trade, because he had made enough to do him and business was getting dull. So he sold me, on credit, his entire stock of goods, amounting to $340. It was a large stock to get on credit, but not difficult to carry. There was a five gallon keg of honey, partly full, billed at $150, a bushel of potatoes at $75, a box of tobacco at $25, and a few other things. It did not take a large counter to display the whole stock. I kept it at night in a box, sunk in the earth, in my shanty, and made my bed over the box at night. So I began trade on what I thought, and what was for that place, a large scale. The money we used was mostly greenbacks. Confederate money was taken at twenty cents on the dollar. All prices were given in the ruling currency, or greenbacks. Potatoes were sold at $75 per bushel, and retailed at from twenty-five to seventy-five cents each, according to size. It was said that one large potato would cure a case of scurvy. Biscuits were bought at $2.50 a dozen, and sold at twenty-five cents each, thirty cents with butter, and thirty-five cents with honey. Eggs retailed at twenty-five cents each; salt, twenty-five cents a spoonful; melons, ten to twenty-five cents a slice, according to the size of the slice; a pint cup of chicken broth, with a spoonful of rice and chicken, shown in the spoon, on top of the cup, forty cents ; huckleberry pies were bought at $1.25 each, and sold at forty cents a quarter. Whiskey

was scarce and hard to find, but now and then a canteen
full would be smuggled in, and it sold for twenty-five
cents for one swallow from the canteen. The prices of
all other goods (and you could buy almost everything
in the provision line, if you had money,) were in the
same proportion. These prices were outrageous, and
the result of the monopoly enjoyed by the prison sutler,
one Selden, formerly of Dubuque, Iowa, and a meaner
rascal than old Wirz knew how to be. No one else was
allowed to sell anything to the prisoners, but a considerable trade was carried on by smugglers, both prisoners
and guards. In order to do anything in the smuggling
line, which was more profitable than legitimate trade, I
secured a prisoner, named James Donahue, who belonged to an Indiana regiment, as a partner. He could
neither read nor write, but was an expert in the smuggling line, and quick and sharp in any kind of trade.
Escape was my hobby, and I spent most of my profits
in various tunnels and other projects for escape, but
never succeeded in getting out, though I was several
times very near success.

When Sherman's army approached Atlanta, the
rebels found that a raid would be made to liberate us,
and began preparations for our removal. Stoneman's
raid was designed for our release, but did not succeed.
On the contrary, a large number of his men were captured, and brought to Andersonville as prisoners.

Instead of rendering any assistance to us, the badly
managed raid of Stoneman resulted in adding several
thousand to the already densely packed prison, making
our condition worse than before. This was not Sher-

man's fault. The plan was a good one, and did credit
both to his head and to his heart. Had others in
authority manifested as much interest in, and consideration for the prisoners, as Sherman did, some arrangement would have been made for their relief.
What a pity that Sheridan, or Kilpatrick, or some man
capable of conducting such a campaign, was not chosen
for the work. No other opportunity for a feat-of-arms
so brilliant as the release of the Andersonville prisoners
would have been, was furnished by the war.

I always have to laugh when I think of Sherman's
scheme for the release of the prisoners. On page 143,
second volume of his Memoirs, he says : " All this time
Hood and I were carrying on the foregoing correspondence relating to the exchange of prisoners, the removal
of the people from Atlanta, and the relief of our prisoners-of-war at Andersonville. Notwithstanding the sev-
erity of their imprisonment, some of these men escaped
from Andersonville and got to me at Atlanta. They
described their sad condition. More than 25,000 prisoners confined in a stockade designed for only 10,000 ;
debarred the privilege of gathering wood out of which
to make huts ; deprived of sufficient healthy food ; and
the little stream that ran through their prison pen poi-
soned and polluted by the offal from their cooking and
butchering houses above. On the 22d of September I
wrote to General Hood describing the condition of our
men at Andersonville, purposely refraining from casting
odium on him or his associates, for the treatment of
these men, but asking his consent for me to procure
from our generous friends at the North the articles of

clothing and comfort which they wanted, viz., under-
clothing, soap, combs, scissors, etc., all needed to keep
them in health, and to send these stores with a train,
and an officer to issue them.   General Hood, on the
24th, promptly consented, and I telegraphed to my
friend, Mr. James E. Yeatman, vice-president of the
Sanitary Commission at St. Louis, to send us all the un-
derclothing and soap he could spare, specifying 1,200
fine-tooth combs and 400 pairs of shears to cut hair.
These articles indicate the plague that most afflicted
our prisoners at Andersonville.

" Mr. Yeatman promptly responded to my request,
expressed the articles, but they did not reach Andersonville in time, for the prisoners were soon after removed.
These supplies did, however, finally overtake them at
Jacksonville, Florida, just before the war closed."

Soap, fine-tooth combs, scissors and underclothes.
What an idea he must have had of our "sad condition,"
when he thought those articles indicated the plague that
most afflicted us.

Uncle Billy, your judgment of the fighting, marching, foraging capacity of a Yankee soldier was never at
fault, but when you proposed to relieve 30,000 starving
Yankees with " 1,200 fine-tooth combs and 400 pairs of
shears," you were away off.   You made no allowance
whatever for Yankee ingenuity.   The soap would have
been handy, the underclothes would have made fine
summer suits, but we were not particular about our appearance.   A starving man will eat before making his
toilet.   There were plenty of fine-tooth combs and
enough shears.   If there hadn't been how long would it

have taken Yankees to have made them ? We were not troubled much with the kind that you can catch with a fine-tooth comb, or cut off with scissors. It was not the fashion there to give away things to eat, but combs and scissors were freely lent. Hard-tack, sow-belly, rice and beans, Uncle Billy, those, and vegetables for scurvy, would have cured us all. Had you been there and seen men make counterfeit greenbacks, make jewelry and mend watches, to say nothing about combs, wooden buckets, and the like, you would laugh yourself at the idea of relieving them with fine-tooth combs and scissors.

One evening, just after dark, I sold something to a prisoner, and gave him change for a $10 greenback. In broad daylight that greenback wouldn't pass, but it was fine work to be done in such a place. I took in trade an open-face silver watch. The crystal got broken. I took it to a watchmaker's shop. He couldn't make a crystal, but he took a silver half-dollar, and with it converted my watch into a hunter case. All such trades were represented there.

When arrangements for our removal were perfected, the old story of a general exchange was again circulated, and was again believed because so much desired. Donahue, my partner, bought a chance to go with the first lot that were taken out; the man who sold the chance staying in Donahue's place. I think the first lot were taken to Savannah and exchanged. When the time came for the detachment to which I belonged to go, I sold out my little stock of goods and concealed in my clothes about seventy dollars in greenbacks that I had accumulated.

We were marched out by detachments. There were so many too weak to walk or so lame from scurvy, that every well man had to assist one or two of the sick or lame to the depot about a mile away. We were halted in front of Wirz's quarters to answer roll-call and be counted. Wirz had been sick, but he came out leaning on a cane, and took occasion to do some of his Dutch swearing. He called us damned Yankee thieves and robbers; said we didn't look so fine as when we came there: was sorry there were so many of us able to go, and that if he had had his way there wouldn't have been a damn man of us alive. I can't remember his words, but that is the substance of his brutal leave-taking.

We were loaded into common cattle-cars and fastened in. Guards with guns rode on the top of each car. At Milledgeville we were unloaded for awhile, and when we were again started from there toward Charleston, we began to feel sure that our prison days were about over. Our hopes revived. We were happy; men who had not smiled for months were brim-full of joy and glee. They forgot hunger, and swollen joints, and fleshless limbs, and useless feet, and talked of blissful hours to come; of meetings soon to be with wives and children, with fathers, mothers, brothers and sisters, and many of " another not a sister." And then the talk would run on things they would get to eat; imaginary tables would be spread, upon which each would place his favorite dish, and all this while crowded together in cattle cars so closely that we had to take turns in lying down. There were no regrets, no mention of past suffering. Hope, bright angel of the morning, ruled in each breast, and to a bright and joyous future each weary eye was turned. Sad, sad, was the sequel.

We reached Charleston, heard the sound of Union guns, even caught a glimpse of the dear old flag. What rejoicing! How we shouted! But presently our train moved on. Our hopes began to sink. When the dismal tidings came that we were on our way to Florence, to another stockade, utter woe and despair took possession where a joyful hope had been.

CHAPTER XIX.

I GO FOR WATER AND ESCAPE—A FAITHFUL PEOPLE—A
NOVEL CHARACTER—A COMICAL HERO.

At Florence, S. C., we were unloaded and placed
on some vacant ground near the depot and a chain of
guards thrown around us.   It was a little before sundown.   I had carried with me a bundle containing a
pair of clean white pants, made of meal bags, and a
white shirt.   Obtaining some water and soap, I washed
myself, put on the clean pants and shirts, and made
myself look as little like a Yankee prisoner as I possibly
could.   I was planning to bribe a guard and get away,
or, if that failed, to knock one over in the dark and run.
I had determined to make at least an effort to escape
before entering another stockade.   I had some sweet
potatoes that I had bought from a negro at a station on
the way, and these I wanted to cook, so as to leave on
a full stomach.

There was a sergeant and squad of guards detailed
to guard the prisoners, from the ground where we were
kept to the well where water was obtained.   I picked
up a bucket to go for water, and got to the place where
an officer was stationed to count out and in those who
went for water.   A little after a gang had passed out, I
spoke politely to the officer and told him I wanted some
water and would at once overtake the party.   They
were but thirty or forty steps away, and he said : " Step
out quick then, and catch up."   I did so in good faith,

and he made another mark on his tally-sheet. I quickly overtook the party, noticing that the officer had turned around as soon as he saw me well up with them, and also that neither the sergeant nor any of the guards had observed my approach. So, instead of falling in behind the column of prisoners, I put on a careless air and walked a little faster, passing both the prisoners and the guards who marched behind them, and walked along in front of the whole party. It occurred to me that the guards might not take me for a Yankee on account of my clothes, and that I could test that point without being chargeable with an attempt to escape. The orders were to shoot any prisoner caught in the act of attempting to escape, and I did not want to run the risk of being shot.

The well that we were going to was in the yard behind the house. I got to it first, filled my bucket and sat down on the back porch of the house, beside the owner of the premises, and commenced talking with him about the Yankee prisoners, conveying the idea that I was not one of them.

The prisoners spent some time in washing themselves before they filled their pails to return. I was in an agony of suspense. I did not know whether the sergeant in charge took me for a prisoner or not, and I dared not undertake to go away until I found out, so I put on as much unconcern as I could, and waited. Finally the order came, " Fall in, Yanks, fall in." The rest formed in line. I paid no attention, but kept on talking to the proprietor. I saw the sergeant looking sharply at me; then he counted his prisoners, and satis-

fied with the count that I was not one, he marched them
away.   I was not with the party when he counted them
out.   My new-made acquaintance was now in the way.
I had to do something with my pail of water or his suspicions would be aroused.   There was no time to spare,
for it was only two hundred yards to where the count-
ing-in would be done by the officer that let me out and
I would be missed; fortunately the man stepped into
the house.   I set my pail of water behind the well-curb,
scaled the high board fence at the back of the yard and
walked off.   I dared not run for that would attract the
attention of people who were in sight.   I got to the
main street where many people were moving back and
forth and talking about the Yanks, and walked away as
fast as I could.   Looking back I saw bayonets glisten-
ing in the rays of the setting sun all around that well
and yard.   I gained the outskirts of the town without
being noticed; got into a patch of woods and then ran
—ran until I felt safe from immediate pursuit, and then
walked on through the woods.

About ten o'clock that night I ran across a party of
negroes hunting possum; I told them who I was, and
asked them about the country, the roads, and the prospects of my getting to Union lines.   They advised me
to make for the coast, and when there, to signal some
blockading vessel.   They said such vessels patrolled the
coast, to prevent the rebels making salt.   I resolved to
follow their advice.   They told me to cross the Pedee
river at a certain ferry, run by a negro whom they said
I could trust.   I found the ferry, and in the morning,
when the negro came out, made myself known to him.

He said it was not safe to travel by day, and took me to a hiding place in the woods, to stay until night, and furnished me with plenty to eat. That night, when he came after me, he brought along another escaped prisoner, a young fellow whose name I have forgotten; he seemed to be all right, and we agreed to stay together. The ferry-man thought our best way was to get a boat, and go down the river to the coast. As there was no moon, he thought we could paddle down by night, without being seen, and hide in the swamps during the day. He told us where we could find a dug-out, and loaned us an iron bar with which to break the lock. We were soon in the dug-out paddling down the Pedee. When morning came I wanted to hide in the woods, but my companion wanted to land at a plantation and get some provisions. We had enough food provided by the ferryman for that day, and I objected to running any unnecessary risks, but he insisted on landing, so I paddled the canoe to the east bank of the river, and stepped out, telling him to go his way, and I would go mine. I never saw him again.

I lay in the brush until toward night, and then started to find some road or plantation before dark, where I could find a negro to give me directions. There was a wide swamp on that side of the river, and not being aware of it, I was soon in it. It was a dismal enough place, full of owls, and bats, and snakes. I traveled several hours in this swamp, and was beginning to think myself in a fix, when I heard a cow-bell, and steering for that, found dry ground. I came to a plantation that night, skulked around until I saw a

negro alone, to whom I told my story. He said that
every white man, woman and child in the county, was
looking for escaped prisoners; that all the bridges and
cause-ways across swamps were guarded at night, and
roads patrolled. The only way I could get through
was to secrete myself during the day and travel with a
negro guide at night, who would know how to avoid
roads and bridges. This negro guided me about ten
miles that night, and left me with one of his friends.
The next day was Sunday, and quite a number of negroes visited me, where I was hid in the woods; they
brought food to give me, and treated me very kindly.
I was the first Union soldier, and probably the first
Union man any of them had ever seen. The questions
they asked were both numerous and novel. I was surprised at their intelligence in some directions, and
amused at their ignorance in others. Their ideas of
government, and of personal and property rights, were
all drawn from the Bible. That was their sole authority,
and they had that down fine. Even those who could
not read, only now and then one could, would quote
passage after passage from the Bible relating to themselves, and give the verse and chapter with surprising
accuracy. Deliverance from slavery was not a surprise
to them; they had been hoping and praying for it for
years, with perfect faith that their prayers would be
answered. It seemed that they had always expected it
to come from some outside source, and had never entertained a thought of taking a part themselves in their
deliverance. They were and are a peculiarly faithful
and patient people. Should they ever become thor-

oughly aroused and united in a movement to throw off
the white man's yoke, that still oppresses and galls
them, I believe that the fortitude, endurance and heroism they will display will surprise the world.

The leader of the company that staid in the woods
with me nearly all that day, was a preacher. Before
he left, seeing that I had no coat, he asked me if I did
not need one, and soon after they went away one of
them came back bringing me quite a comfortable overcoat. That night I was guided to a plantation on a
public road running from Florence to a place on the
coast where there were salt works. There a plan was
formed of secreting me in a wagon that made weekly
trips to the coast, driven by a negro. I waited two days
for the wagon, concealed in the daytime in a fodder
house, under the bundles of corn fodder. When the
negro came along with his wagon he had two passengers, a white woman and her little girl. Of course I
could not ride in such company.

That night I was piloted again through woods and
swamps and left at the house of a negro preacher. He
lived alone, and when he went to work locked his door
with a padlock on the outside, leaving me on the inside.
He procured for me some paper, pen and ink, and I
wrote myself a rebel furlough, thinking it might come
handy should I be picked up by some of the patrols. I
represented myself in the furlough as belonging to the
Georgia regiment that had guarded us from Andersonville to Florence, and I signed the name of a captain
whom I happened to know. That night there was no one
ready to guide me further, and I was taken to a stack of

straw out in a field, into which I crawled to spend the night. Along in the night someone came and crawled into the straw quite close to me. I thought it must be a negro, but said nothing. About daylight I heard my unknown bed-fellow crawling out, and concluded to crawl out too, and see who he was. We were both badly scared when we stood up and faced each other. He was a rebel soldier in full uniform. He had deserted and was hiding in the neighborhood of his home, making occasional visits by stealth to his family. I bought this man's jacket, which had South Carolina buttons, for $5 in greenbacks.

That day I was secreted in the woods, and when my dinner was brought to me at noon, a big negro with a club and a gun, accompanied the bearer. He was a run-away slave. Had been in the woods and swamps for seven years. Had often been pursued but never captured. Said that white men could not take him alive. He roamed about from place to place, occasionally visiting his wife and children. He was known to most of the negroes in the regions he frequented, and by them had never been betrayed. He killed hogs and cattle, and traded the meat to other negroes for clothing and bread. He was a veritable wild man of the woods, and the story of his adventures and escapes from bloodhounds entertained and thrilled me for hours.

That night I secured a guide and moved on. Was left at another plantation, where I staid two days to let an old uncle mend my shoes.

Provided with another faithful guide, I passed through a wide swamp, crossing the deep creeks on a foot-path of logs known only to negroes. Over the swamp I was directed to a plantation some miles away, where I was to wake up another negro in a certain one of the negro houses that was described. It was a bright moonlight night, and I did not feel safe on a public road, so I stopped at the first plantation I came to, thinking it better to trust the first negro I could find than to go alone.

I knocked at what I supposed was a negro quarter. At first no answer. I rapped louder, and a voice called out: "Who is there?" It was unquestionably a white man's voice. I replied: "I'm a stranger, have lost my way and want to stay all night." And then I ran. Was out of sight by the time he had slipped on his pants and opened the door. I ran on until I came to the forks of two roads. Here there was a solitary log house. I crept up to it, and peering through a crack, saw two negroes sitting in front of the fireplace. They were talking, and, thinking I could form an opinion from their talk as to whether they would do for me to trust, I watched them and listened. Presently I heard the galloping of a horse up the road I came, and had just time to hide in the shadow of some scrub oaks near by, when a white man came up at full gallop, revolver in hand. He rapped at the door and brought the negroes out, saying: "Bring out that white rascal you have got hid in there." They had seen no white man and told him to come in and search, which he did.

He then galloped away, taking the same road I wanted to follow. I did not like the appearance of the two negroes, and so ran on after my pursuer. He stopped at every plantation, and made inquiries, and I usually came up about the time he would be leaving. I followed him in this way until I came to the plantation that I had been directed to, and counting off so many houses from the white folks' house, and whispering his name at a crack between the logs, attracted the atten·tion of the negro that I was after. He had been awakened by the noise made by the man on the horse. He was wonderfully tickled at the idea of my following the man who was pursuing me. (This negro advised me to stay with him until the negro from Florence, with the wagon, came along again. Said he would be there on the next night, on his way to the coast, and would stay all night with him. I stayed concealed in the woods. The negro with the wagon was on time, and early the following morning I was carefully stored away in the wagon underneath the fodder carried to feed the mules. It was a covered wagon, and full of the fodder of that country, which is the leaves stripped from corn, cured and tied in bundles. The wagon was drawn by three mules. The driver rode on the nigh wheel mule, and drove the leader with a jerk-line.

I have seen many attempts to imitate the negro, but here was an original and comic genius that beat any negro minstrel I have ever seen. He had a banjo, a fiddle and a pair of bones. He wore a fireman's hat, made of leather and iron, and was otherwise rigged out in clownish fashion. At nearly every house we passed he had something to deliver. Packages of goods, purchased at Florence, letters and messages. His wagon seemed to be a kind of weekly express for all the coun-

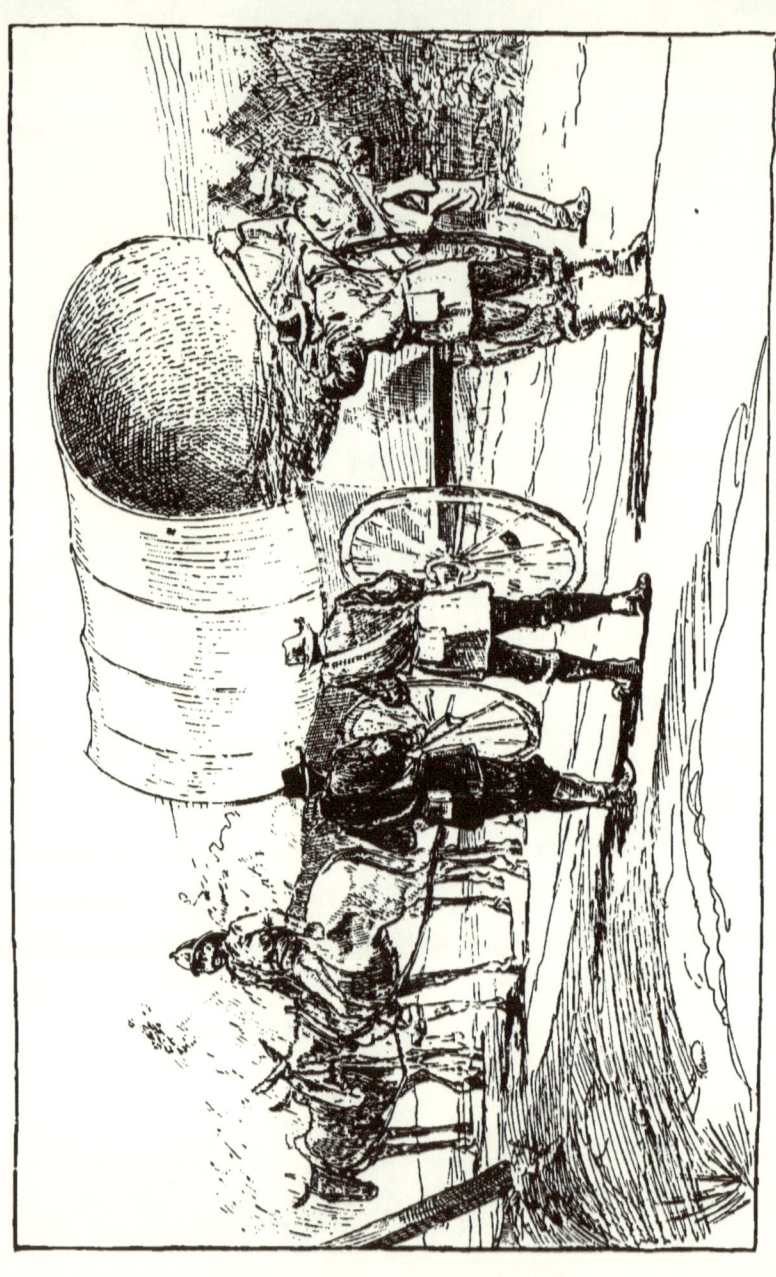

IF YOU'UNS THOUGHT DAH WAS YANKS IN DIS WAGON, I COULD JIS DANCE JUBA ON YOU-ALLS COAT TAILS.

try through which he passed. Every one knew him, and every one bantered and joked with him. As he drove along the road he whistled, and sang, and played on his several instruments in turn.

At Conwayborough, a village through which we passed, there was a bridge and some rebel soldiers on guard. The negro bantered and joked with them also, and when they asked him if he had any Yanks in his wagon, he replied, "Go way dah—you home guards— you 'uns thought dah was Yanks in dis here wagon, I could jus dance juba on you 'uns coat tails as dey'd stick out behind." The rebels thought best to make some search, and they poked the fodder around with the muzzles of their guns. As for me, I was so badly scared that I thought they must surely hear the rattle of the fodder caused by the beating of my heart. They discovered nothing, and we moved on.

When there were no houses in sight I crawled out of my hole in the fodder, and watched the road behind us, the driver watching in front. And thus with music and song, gibes and jokes, and juba danced on the saddle of the nigh mule, we journeyed to the sea.

About 10 o'clock that night we began to hear the sound of the breakers. I had never seen the sea, and supposed that when it was calm there were no waves. This was a beautiful, calm, moonlight night, and to hear the roar of breakers two miles away was a revelation to me. I had thought all along that I would take a great bath when I came to the sea, and when we got there I undressed and walked out on the sandy beach, but those breakers I had not counted on, and I dared not venture in.

CHAPTER XX.

My comical guide made me known to some of the darkies at the salt works. They kept me concealed and took care of me several days, but thought there was not much prospect of my getting away in a blockade vessel; said the blockaders had ceased to visit that part of the coast. I remained there until I got tired of waiting and watching, and then, after consulting with the best posted of the negroes, concluded to work my way into Wilmington, N. C., and if possible enlist on a blockade runner. These darkies had heard that it was so hard to get men to go on blockade runners that the officers would take whoever applied, without asking questions.

My idea was that if I could get on one of these vessels, and did not get captured by my friends, I could claim protection from an American Consul at some neutral port, where the vessel would land. I was near the line between North and South Carolina, and one night I started up the coast toward Wilmington. About 12 o'clock I came to a stream or inlet where there was a ferry. There was a plantation on the side of the stream that I was on, and quite a number of negro houses. I entered one of these, the door of which was open, and after pulling and shaking him for some time,

awakened a negro who lay on the floor, with his feet to
the fireplace, in which there was a fire burning. He
turned out to be a pure African, born in Africa, and I
could not get much out of him; in fact, could not understand much of his jargon. While trying to talk with
this man, two other negroes came in who had been out
hunting. From them I learned that the plantation belonged to Captain ——; that he was suspected of being
a Union man; that he had sold all his slaves before the
war began, and that he was originally from the state of
Maine; had been captain of a vessel engaged in ship-
ping; owned the plantation and was working it with
hired negroes; also that there was a small fort just
across the inlet or stream, and some rebel soldiers there.

Pondering these things, it occurred to me that it
would do to trust this white man. So I went to his
house and rapped on his door. At first I got no answer.
Rapping harder, some one called out, "Who's there?"
I replied, "I am a stranger, and want to see Mr. ——."
I listened with my ear at the door, heard him get up
and dress, and thought I heard him getting down a gun.
Anyway, my courage failed me as I thought of the fix
I would be in if he should open the door gun in hand.
In that case it would be all right if he turned out to be
a Union man, and all wrong otherwise. And just then
it occurred to me that a Union man would not have
been permitted to remain alive in that country, and
that I didn't want to see a man that was so long getting
ready to open his door. When he did open it I was not
there, I had changed my mind and was making double-
quick time for a bridge that the darkies said crossed

the stream some miles up from that place. Their direction was to take the main road until I came to a road turning off to the right. I did so, and after following the road that turned off to the right two or three miles, it gave out and I found it only to be a wood road. Retracing my steps, I got into the main road and followed it to where a second road turned off to the right; followed that two or three miles with the same success as before, and when I got back to the main road again it was broad daylight, and I was still in sight of that plantation. In fact, was on a part of it, and looking through the cracks of a log house, saw two negro women sleeping on the floor, and one up, cooking breakfast.

Being tired and hungry, I asked the woman to let me in. She objected at first, but when I told her I was a Union soldier escaped from prison, she unlocked the door and let me in. I told her I had been traveling all night and would like something to eat. I wish I could repeat verbatim all that woman said. Her home was in Georgia, where she had a family of children from whom she had been taken and sent as a hired hand to work on this plantation. Her whole soul was up in arms against the whole white race. She give me something to eat! No; if one mouthful of her bread would keep every white man on earth from starving, she wouldn't give it. I asked her why she had let me in, and tried to explain that I was a Union soldier, and that Union soldiers were friends of the slaves. No use. She had let me in because she wanted a chance to speak her mind to a white man, whom she had no cause to fear; and she improved the opportunity by cursing and emptying the vials of her wrath on me as a substitute for the whole white race. Hers was the most cutting abuse I ever heard from human tongue, and withal, she displayed facility in the use of words and a kind of rude eloquence. I offered to pay her for something to eat. She would rather turn a white man from her door hungry than to have all the money on earth. I asked her if she was going to tell her master that I had been there? No, she wouldn't do anything to please her master, and receiving this assurance I was glad to be turned hungry from her door. She was the only one of the race I ever applied to in vain for assistance.

I had until this avoided traveling alone by day, but now saw no way of finding and crossing the bridge except by daylight. After resting and sleeping awhile in the woods, I started again to find the bridge. Where there was timber on both sides of the road, I followed the road walking in the edge of the woods, watching warily, and ready to hide behind trees should I meet or see anyone. About noon I met a negro boy and asked him about roads, plantations, negroes, and such things as I wanted to know, without telling him who I was. I made a blunder in saying to him as he rode away, not to tell any white man that he had seen me. Now, it happened that I was passing through that neighborhood, or trying to pass through, on the very day set by the planters for a grand hunt with dogs and guns, after a lot of rebel deserters who infested the region, concealing themselves in swamps by day, and preying on pig-pens, hen-roosts and whatever else they could steal by night. The negroes were not more friendly to this

class of marauders than the whites were. The negro
boy I talked with took me for one of these deserters,
and immediately rode to where his master and other
white men had assembled, and put them on my track.

Near where I met the boy, there was a log house in
the middle of a corn field. The boy told me it was an
old negro's quarters. When the boy was out of sight I
went into a school house near the road on my right, and
there left my overcoat and a little bundle, in which I
had some fat bacon and some raw sweet potatoes, concealed under a desk. I then crossed the road and went
to this negro quarter. The old negro had seen me meet
the boy, and he was much alarmed when I told him my
story. He feared the boy would report me. He gave
me some raw fish and bread and a little fire between
two pieces of bark, and directed me to a place in the
swamp, across the field, where I could, he thought, build
a small fire and not be found unless the dogs should
take my track, in which case, he said, I should be sure
to be caught whether I stopped or not. He did not
think the dogs would follow a white man's track.

I built a small fire and roasted my fish, which were
from the salt water,—mullets, I think, and the finest fish
I ever tasted. Dinner over, I took a nap, and when I
awoke started back to the negro hut, but not following
the path by which I had come. The old man saw me
coming and met me in the corn. He was the most complete picture of fright that you can possibly imagine.
His hair literally stood straight up—woolly hair at that.
His teeth chattered and his black face seemed to be an
ash color. He was so much agitated that at first I

could not understand his rapidly uttered jargon. Finally he made me understand that the white men were
after me, had been to his house, and were on my track
into the woods. He wanted me to go with him and
give myself up. " Oh, Massa," he said, " if da' do n't
ketch you, da' skin dis nigga alive. Da' done tie dis
nigga up an whip him to def." I quieted his fears as
much as I could, and hastened across the corn field to
the school house. My coat and bundle were gone. I
surmised that the dogs not being trained for that purpose, would not track a white man, and that it would be
better to hide than to travel and take chances of being
seen.

Not far off there was an abandoned field with deep
gullies washed through, and in the gullies and on their
sides a thick matting of blackberry briers, vines and
brush. I made my way to this field, taking care to leave
no tracks that could be seen, and hid in one of the ra-
vines. There I could plainly hear the tooting of horns
and the sound of voices calling to the hounds. The
negro was right; the hounds were not trained for white
man's track.

I started again about midnight, moving stealthily
through woods and fields on a line with the road. In
about two hours I reached the river again that I wanted
to cross. I knew the bridge was near, but I feared a
guard might be there, and I made a bundle of my
clothes, intending to tie them on top of my head and
swim across. As I sat on the bank in the moonlight
wondering if I could swim well enough to reach the
other shore, I saw something disturb the water—a large

fish or an alligator. All thought of getting into that water vanished. I put on my clothes and crept cautiously from tree to tree, along the bank, until I could see the bridge. I crawled up close to it and watched and listened. I lay there half an hour or more. I could neither hear nor see anything to indicate that a guard was there. Thinking that if there should be a guard there, it would be better for me to be stopped walking carelessly along than to be caught trying to slip over, especially as I meant to play the furlough dodge if I should be taken, I slipped back into the woods, stepped into the road some distance from the bridge, and came whistling along to the bridge. Was half way over and breathing freer, when a boy stepped from behind a large tree in front of me, and called out, "Halt!" He was but twenty rods away, and I could see plainly that he was a mere boy, but he held a dangerous weapon, a double-barreled shot-gun. I could see that both barrels were cocked, and that boy or no boy, he meant business. "Well, my boy," I said, "what do you want?" "About, face!" "You must be a raw recruit," I said. "You ought to say, ' Who goes there?' if I say, 'Friend!' then you should say, ' Advance and give the countersign!' " " You about face," said he, " or I'll shoot!" and he leveled his gun. There was no other way to do, and I turned around. "Forward, march!" was his next command. I tried to talk to him and get him to look at my furlough, but he would have none of it, and answered nothing, except " Forward, march !" and " Go right along, or I'll shoot!" And forward, march, it was; captured by a fourteen-year-old boy that I could have

CAPTURED BY A FOURTEEN-YEAR-OLD BOY.

dropped over the bridge with one hand, could I have prevailed on him to come within my reach. We marched
back about half a mile, the boy keeping well behind
with cocked gun, when we met his brother-in-law, on
horseback, coming to relieve him. The brother-in-law
was a lieutenant of artillery, and at home on a furlough.
They marched me back to their father's house which
was near where I had been hunted the day before. On
the way, I learned that they took me for a deserter, and
that when the crowd gathered the next day I was liable
to be hung, or whipped severely at the best, and sent to
the front. Under these circumstances I thought it best
to show my colors, so I told them I was a prisoner of
war trying to escape. When we got into the house I
was given a seat near the fire-place and managed to slip
my furlough into the fire without being seen.

It was hard to make these people believe that I was
a Union soldier. They said I talked and looked like a
Southerner. I told them it was easy enough for me to
talk and act like a Southern man, because my parents
were Kentuckians, and both my grandfathers, Virgin-
ians, and that when I tried to play the rebel soldier, as
I was trying until they talked about ropes and whips,
all I had to do was to fall back on my mother tongue.

The owner of this place was an ideal Southern man,
manners, chivalry and all. He scouted the idea of mis-
treating a prisoner. "This young man," said he, "was
a gentleman at home, and in my house he shall be
treated as a guest." There were in the family two
daughters, two sons, and the son-in-law, who was at
home on a furlough.

When breakfast time came, these young people seemed to object to eating at the same table with a Yankee soldier. "Then turn him loose," said the old man. "No white man whose ancestors are from Kentucky and Virginia shall be forced to sit here while we eat, and not be offered a seat at the table." I tried to make some excuse, not caring to sit at a table where there were those who objected, but the old gentleman would take no excuses. "If you were my boy," he said, ' you would be in the rebel army. You live in the North, and you would be a traitor to your home if you were not on the Union side."

After breakfast my boy captor was sent on a horse to the fort at the mouth of the river, and brought back two soldiers who took me to the fort. The next day was Sunday, and hundreds of people, both white and black, came to take their first look at a Yankee soldier. I was kept there several days, and then sent along with several guards and some loaded wagons to Whiteville, a place on a railroad between Florence and Wilmington.

We arrived at this place on Saturday morning after the train to Florence had passed, and I had to remain until Monday, and was turned over to the provost marshal. This gentleman treated me very kindly, walked around the town with me for awhile, and took me to his house to tea.

When night came, however, he said he would have to lock me up in the county jail. I objected to this, and tried hard to persuade him to either put a guard over me, or take my parole of honor and keep me at his house.

He would not yield, and into the jail, behind the bars of a common felon's cell, I had to go. It had been humiliating to be captured by a fourteen-year-old boy; to be locked in a felon's cell, although charged with no crime, broke me all up; I felt that it was a disgrace; I lay down on the straw mattress in the cell and cried like a child.

The next morning when a jailor came in with food for the prisoners, he laid on a mantel, separated by the corridor from my cell, a fine butcher knife. It was about six feet from the bars of my cage. It would, I thought, be a fine prize if I could get it and take it with me back to prison. The only articles in my cell were the mattress and the southern substitute for a broom. This was made of a bunch of some kind of long grass, the butts wound with a cord, forming the handle, the tops forming the broom. Grasping this by the tops of the straws, I could reach through the bars and touch the knife. Working the knife around until the point was towards me, and the end of the handle against the wall, I pushed the handle of the broom against the point of the knife until I had it fast, then drew it into the cell. When the jailor came along, the bunch of straw was lying on the floor of the cell, the knife concealed in it, and I was innocently eating my breakfast. "I left a knife on that mantel, who took it?" he said. I looked up. "Who took that knife?" "I am sure there has been no one there since you passed," I replied. He went back and searched; came again, looked into my cell, tried the door of the corridor, and found it locked as he left it. He remarked to me, "You couldn't get that knife if I did leave it there, I must have taken it with me, and some of them damn niggers have got it." The other prisoners were all negroes. He went back and searched again, then went out, saying that he had either left that knife outside, or else the jail was haunted.

I was taken out on Monday and conveyed on the cars to Florence, where I was searched before being sent to the stockade, and the knife found. I told the officer who found it, where and how I got it, and asked him to return it to that jailor with my compliments.

Here let me remark, that from the time I was recaptured in North Carolina, until I was delivered back at Florence, I saw and talked with many people, both soldiers and citizens, and received only such treatment as a soldier taken in honorable warfare ought to receive at the hands of his captors, except, perhaps, being put in a felon's cell, which may have been a matter of necessity, rather than intentional degradation.

CHAPTER XXI.

The return to a stockade I had very much dreaded, because I supposed I would have to endure tortures similar to those to which escaped prisoners brought back at Andersonville were subjected. Whatever of fortitude I possessed was not of the kind that enables a man to endure physical pain. I was agreeably surprised on reaching the prison, to find that to be hand-cuffed, and my hand-cuffs fastened to those of five or six other prisoners, and to remain in this somewhat uncomfortable position forty-eight hours without food, was the only punishment I was to receive. That was so much milder than I expected, that it really seemed no punishment at all.

The forty-eight hours having expired, one Lieutenant Barrett came to release us and turn us into the stockade. He was a brute and a coward. Noticing my gray jacket, he swore that no damn Yankee should disgrace the uniform of South Carolina. I remarked that it was cold weather to wear nothing but a shirt. "Come with me," he said with brutal oaths, "I'll get a coat for you." He led me to the dead house, a kind of shed made with forks and poles, and covered and enclosed with brush.

There were several corpses in there, each having on an old pair of drawers or ragged pants and a worn-out blue blouse. "There," he said, "go in there and get a uniform; those Yanks are all in hell already and don't need any clothes." I told him that I would rather get along without any coat than to take one from a dead body. "None of your talk to me!" he replied. "Go in there and get one of those blouses." He drew and cocked his revolver as he spoke. To take a coat from a cold, stiff corpse, was no easy task. I finally got one off; the inside was white in places with lice. The sight of it made me sick. "Put it on!" he roared. I held it up and said, "Lieutenant, look at it, let me have a chance to clean it first?" I stood in reach of him, and the thought that I could knock him down and run came into my mind just as a rebel sergeant, who stood near, and who had on a blue jacket, spoke up and said: "See here, lieutenant, let me take that gray jacket and give the Yank this blue one. I'd like mighty well to make such a trade." The brute evidently did not like to have a witness to his intended and needless brutality, and he reluctantly yielded.

All survivors of Florence will remember that Barrett. They hated him worse, if anything, than they ever did Wirz. He seemed to take delight in subjecting prisoners to every kind of insult, humiliation and cruelty whenever he could find or make an excuse for doing so. It was well for us that he was not in full charge as Wirz had been.

The Florence stockade was the old Andersonville stockade duplicated. It was built the same way, the same dead-line, the lay of land, creek, and swamp, all the same. It contained about twelve acres and about

12,000 prisoners. The new prisoners brought there thought it a horrible place, but those from Andersonville did not complain. They had gone in when there were boughs and brush enough to enable them to build little huts, and they knew how. The rations were the same in quantity, but better in quality. They were issued raw, and wood furnished to cook with. Some clothing and blankets, though not nearly enough to go round, were sent by some sanitary relief committee from the North, and distributed. It was said that a suit of clothes and a pair of blankets were sent for every man, but not one-tenth of that amount was distributed to the prisoners. Colonel Iverson, who was in command at Florence, although a strict disciplinarian, was, I believe, a gentleman at heart. He seemed to do as well by us as circumstances would permit, and so far as I know, was never charged with personal cruelty.

On being turned into the stockade, I was taken into a shanty by two of the boys from my regiment who had kept the blankets and cooking outfit that I had left when I got away. Life with me for a few weeks was again about the same as at Andersonville, except that I had some money and could piece out my scanty rations and not actually suffer from hunger. Money among the prisoners had become scarce, and consequently trade was neither brisk nor profitable. I tried keeping a stand, but could not make anything out of it.

One morning an officer came in to get fifty prisoners to go out on parole of honor and chop wood for the prison. I had never chopped a cord of wood in my life, but wanted to be in the fresh air, so I managed to get taken out as a chopper.

We were taken to the front of the colonel's tent. Our names taken, we held up our hands and took an oath that we would not violate our parole by going over a certain distance from the prison, nor by failing to return at the proper time every night. We were furnished with axes and sent to the woods.

The men divided into pairs, each pair had to cut two cords per day; the timber to be cut was on some swampy land about half a mile from the prison. I happened to be paired with a man from Maine, a thorough woodsman and a good chopper. He soon discovered that I couldn't chop. My hands were blistered, and I was completely tuckered at the end of an hour. I said to him: "Partner, you see I can't keep up my end at this work, but there are persimmons in the woods around here, and cornfields with beans in the corn. I am some on beans and persimmons, and if you will do the chopping, I will pile the wood and divide persimmons and beans." He agreed. We had persimmons for dinner and our pockets full of beans to take back when we went in at night. The officers soon got on to the bean racket and searched us every night, taking everything of that kind away.

They permitted each man to carry in with him a stick of wood at night, and we managed to get hollow logs to carry in and conceal our plunder in them. One evening they discovered this game. We had come to the prison gate, laid down our loads of wood in front of the officers' tents, and were waiting to get our extra rations before going in. One of the men laid down a long hollow stick, full of beans. One of the officers was out of wood, and told his negro servant to take one of our logs. The negro happened to take the log that had the beans, and as he cut it, the beans rolled out and the officer saw them. After that the search at night included hollow logs.

Besides the fifty choppers, one man was paroled as captain and another as clerk. Richard Wardell was the clerk. He and myself had been companions in daily rambles after beans and persimmons. In fact, our motto was: " Whatever your hands find to take let them take." One day Wardell told me that he had secured. a better job, and he resigned the clerkship in my favor. At the same time he gave me a pocket memoranda to keep the roll of the choppers in. This book and a ten cent piece of script money are my only relics of prison life.

It was now some time in December. Commencing Christmas, I kept a memoranda in this book, some of which I copy, because they show prison life as I saw it there.

" *Dec. 25, 1864.* To-day is the fourth Christmas I have spent away from home; may it be the last. The colonel said that as it was Sunday and Christmas too, we might have holiday and not go out to chop. Quite a favor, indeed, to be allowed to spend the principal holiday in the year in the most miserable hole on the face of the earth. Other days I go out on a parole of honor to chop wood for the prison. There are fifty-two in the chopping squad, including the captain of the squad and myself. The remuneration we receive is one pound of meal or rice and a half pound of beef per day, which it is my duty to draw and issue to the rest. The ration we draw in camp is one pound of meal and a little salt, with now and then a small quantity of beans or potatoes. I ate for breakfast to-day some rice and potatoes; for dinner, rice and meal dumplings, and will have some supper if we get rations to-day. Have just been to the gate to draw rations, but the rebels say we cannot have any to-day, because we did not work. There is a report here that Jeff Davis is dead, which is generally believed. There were some more galvanized Yanks turned in to-day. They were prisoners who took the oath of allegiance to the confederacy and went into the rebel army, but were so no-account that the rebels wouldn't have them.

"*Dec. 26, 1864.* We are out in the swamp to-day. It rained last night, and the water is so high that the men can scarcely work. It is as warm here to-day as it is in May in Wisconsin. From all appearances, our days of confinement will soon be over. It is reported that Sherman is marching on Charleston. If he is, he will surely take it, and then it will be easy for him to send a raid here and release us.

"*Dec. 27, 1864.* The rebs had their flag pole raised to-day that the Yankee sailors had been making for them. They made some of the prisoners raise it for them. I think it will not be long before there will be a Yankee flag flying on it. Our boys came a good joke on them while they were having it raised, which will not do to be written. I succeeded in getting Carr out

to-day to make axe-helves. He will commence to-
morrow."

The joke was this. While the men were chopping
in the swamp, a fat steer came trotting through the
woods, and scared by the noise of the axes he stopped
near a tall Tennesseean who was standing on a log.
The Tennesseean reached over and tapped him behind
the horns with his axe. He dropped dead. We skinned
and dressed him and divided the meat among the choppers. Knowing that we would be searched at night,
and that hollow logs were played out, I devised this
scheme to carry in the meat. The former captain of
the squad had been sent away with some of the sick
who were to be exchanged, and I had been given his
place. I had two or three skilful axemen prepare logs
of ash, the kind we usually carried in, and cut them exactly alike at each end, leaving as much uncut as could
be broken. When broken, the splintered part of the
ends where they were broken, came opposite each
other. The logs were then carefully split so that the
splintered part of each end was divided. The two
halves were then hollowed out, making two troughs.
These were then filled with steer and then the two
parts carefully put together and fastened with small
wedges at the end, put in across the split end. We
arranged enough of these logs to carry all the steer, except the feet, head and such other parts as we used for
dinner that day. There was no sign of a crack in these
logs, and the boys who carried them, to prevent the discovery of the wedges that held them together at the
ends, let the ends down in the muddy places when they

stopped to rest.   We were properly searched that night,
but the steer got through.   Every night after that the
ash logs, that had been prepared to carry in beans, and
such other things as the boys secured, were laid in some
appointed place, and I inspected them, allowing none
to go in unless skilfully prepared.   This game was not
discovered while I was there.

"*Dec. 28, 1864.*   Rained all the forenoon.   The boys
wanted to go in.   Colonel Iverson said they might go,
but they would have to stay, and he would get men to
chop who could stand a little rain.   We stayed, and
were all soaked to the skin.   Chopping wood in a cold
chilly rain for a pint of corn-meal a day is tough.   But
a pint of corn-meal, added to our prison ration, keeps
the gnawing wolf, Hunger, from the stomach.   Besides,
we are allowed to take in, at night, as much wood as
we can carry, and what we get by selling, or trading
our wood, added to our double ration of meal, enables
us to live quite comfortably, as far as food and fuel go.
Like kings compared to those, the common herd, the
15,000 who are trying to eke out existence on a scant
pint of meal and a small stick of wood per day.

"We are called the chopping squad.   Another
squad, called the carrying squad, 200 in number, carry
into the prison the wood that we chop.   Each man has
to carry on his back a quarter of a cord, each day, of
green wood an average distance of one-half mile; and
much of the way over a bridge, made of single foot
logs, that crosses the swamp.   The carriers are paid the
same as the choppers.   They have one sergeant in
charge of each hundred, and another to act as commis-

sary—that is, to draw and issue the pint of meal to each man; and another, called captain, who commands the squad.

"The other day some prisoners managed to flank out with the carrying squad, and escape. Whether they were aided or not by the captain or sergeants is not known, but to-day the captain and sergeants are in the dungeon; their men are left inside, and there is an entirely new gang on the foot logs. Succeeded to-day in getting my friend, Horace C. Carr, paroled to make axe handles for our squad. He made six good handles. Says he can make them faster when he gets used to having enough to eat.

"*Dec. 29, 1864.* Has been a cold, windy day. The 'rebs' hoisted their flag on the new pole. Judging from their actions, they cannot have much respect for nor much faith in their cause. They stood around the pole with their hands in their pockets, and did not say a word, or offer to cheer when the flag went up. The Yanks in the stockade greeted it with loud groans and hisses. The body, or main part of this flag, is white. In the upper corner, next the pole, there is a red square, and across this red square there are blue bars with white border. On the bars there are thirteen stars.

"*Dec. 30, 1864.* Has been a pleasant day, bright and balmy and warm. This is the Sunny South that we read about. Went with Dick Wardell on a little ramble into the country. Guess we stretched the limits of our parole. Stopped at a house to get a drink, and some ladies, who were there, talked with us quite awhile and were very polite. They asked us to come again next week, and bring a ring that we have to sell, and an album, if we could get one. We promised to do so. Was thinking to-day, as we returned, how much our prison life resembles the life of brutes. The horse, for instance, which is transferred from one place to another, and will go to and from each new stable, seldom making an effort to return to the old. So with us. Separated from friends and home, we are moved about from place to place, and still, our walk over, it seems perfectly natural to turn to the stockade, where we have not as good as a manger to be stabled in. There is a rumor to-day that we are to be moved to Columbia. If we are, I shall make another attempt to gain my liberty. Would rather make my escape, and get to our lines, than receive a thousand dollars and be exchanged.

"*Sat., Dec. 31, 1864.* Cold and chilly, with some rain. Old Father Time seems to be dragging a heavy load; he moves so slow. Prospects for the new year gloomy enough. Could we poor mortals but lift the veil of uncertainty that seems to hang like a pall between us and the future, we might see beyond brighter and happier days; and we might see beyond (surely, some would) that which would blanch the cheek with terror and kill the little courage we have. Better, perhaps, the ills we have than the evils we know not of. In an uncertain future there is a chance for hope at least, to all. 'The New Year comes to-night, mamma,' and this will be the fourth time it has come and found your boy away. May God grant that ere the close of it, he may be restored to you and home.

"*New Year, 1865.* Fine morning. Air clear and

cold. Ground frozen. Last New Year's I was in my snug winter quarters at Vicksburg, enjoying, what I now recall as the comforts and blessings of freedom in a civilized land, and what I then considered the necessary hardships of a soldier's life. Thus ' Blessings brighten as they take their flight.'

"For dinner George and I had a pie, made of boiled beef and flour dumplings. George, my bunk-mate, is a nurse in a hospital. He has been getting flour for his extra ration. I have been getting beef instead of meal. We have been saving our flour and beef for three days, and we have had for this place a grand dinner. We kept a blanket over the front of our mansion while we ate, so that our hungry neighbors might not stare at us with starving eyes."

Here follows an inventory of my worldly effects, the chief of which was a two-dollar greenback, then an inventory of bad habits, the chief of which was swearing; then moral reflections and promises of reform. Don't conclude from this that I was then a democrat.

"*Jan. 2, 1865.* Out with the chopping squad, as usual. Sold Brunt's watch to-day to one of the rebel cavalrymen, for $1.25 in money and $1.15 in trade.

"*Jan. 3, 1865.* Lovely day. Air as soft and balmy as a May morning in God's country. Such days warm my blood, and make me feel cagey. Have been thinking up plans of escape all day. Went over to see the lady who wanted the ring. She said she had spent all her money and couldn't take it. Guess she isn't much of a lady after all. Believe she is a kind of a camp-follower.

" The fine weather has had a bad effect on the paroled men. Thirteen of them skipped out to-day. One
of them, James Coon, belonged to our squad. I expect
we will all lose our job."

The James Coon, mentioned above, was one of the
party with whom I was handcuffed when I was brought
back, after my first attempt to escape. He had been
trying for several days to induce me to run away with
him, in violation of our parole of honor. Although I
was always thinking and planning escape I did not like
the idea of violating a parole. Technically and literally considered, I had never been paroled. When the
chopping squad was first called for, and taken out to
be paroled, the rebel officer, who had charge of the
matter, formed us in double line, and then proceeded
to take down each man's name. He wrote one or two
names, and then to expedite matters, called for one of
us to do the job of writing. Several of us stepped out,
and I was chosen. I stood beside the officer and wrote
each name that was given him and repeated to me.
When the roll was complete he ordered the men in the
line to hold up each his right hand, and take an oath,
called the parole of honor. I stood beside the officer,
facing the prisoners, and did not hold up my hand ; did
not think of it at the time, and the officer did not notice
me. Hence, I was not, in fact, paroled. Coon knew
of it, and used that as an argument to persuade me to
go with him. Whether it is justifiable, under any circumstances, for a man to violate such an oath of honor
in order to escape from captors, is a moral problem not
easy of solution. Of course, if prisoners-of-war were

receiving honorable treatment there could be no excuse or justification for one who would violate a parole, voluntarily taken. But just how much unnecessary, unjustifiable and unusual cruelty a man must suffer, before he would be justified in breaking a parole to get away, that is a question. " Thou shalt not kill," is a command of God, and a law of every civilized people. But in no civilized nation is a man required to lose his own life rather than to take that of his assailant.

Coon started soon after we got into the woods that morning. I was at that time captain of the chopping squad. As Coon had confided his plans to me I could not betray him, although I knew that his going would, in all probability, result in all the rest of us losing our places. That meant more than the loss of a pint of meal a day; it meant that we must stay in the stockade, with the rest of the prisoners, and live on a pint of meal a day. It diminished the chances for life to all of us. None of the choppers, except myself, knew that he was going. He was not missed until the noon roll-call, which I was required to make each day. Then the boys supposed he had gone after beans or persimmons. About 2 o'clock I went to Colonel Iverson's quarters, and told him that one of my men was missing at roll-call. Coon had consented that I should report him at that time, in order, if possible, to save myself from the dungeon, and the rest of the boys from being left inside. My diary discloses the result.

CHAPTER XXII.

PAROLE OF HONOR PLAYED OUT—A SCHEME FOR ESCAPE—
ALL IS FAIR IN LOVE AND WAR — BRIBING A YANKEE
WITH A REBEL'S MONEY—I GO AFTER SHAKES AND DO
NOT RETURN.

"*Jan 4, 1865.* Weather fine to-day, but it rained last night, giving the boys who ran away a good chance to elude the dogs. Our squad was not taken out to-day. None of the paroled men went out. George will sleep at the hospital hereafter, and I will be alone in the shanty. Lost $20 of confederate money last night. It must have been stolen.

"Had a very strange dream. Thought I had, in some way, escaped and got home. When I entered the house all our family, and uncle's family, and many of the young people of the neighborhood were there. They all gathered around me and began to talk, and tried to shake hands with me, but I pushed them all aside, and ran to mother and kissed her, and was so overcome with joy that I laid my head in her lap and wept for a long time. Then I shook hands with the rest, telling them it was the happiest day of my life. It would have been.

"*Jan. 5, 1865.* Parole of honor played out. New squads are being organized. None of the old hands are allowed to go. Colonel Iverson came in to see about the new men for parole, I asked him to let me have charge of the choppers again. He refused, but said I

might go as a chopper, if I liked. I told him I could not
chop a cord of wood a day, and that if he did not let me
out as before, I would try to escape. He said: 'All
right, my boy, you are welcome to try.'"

I did try. Although I wrote memoranda each day
I could not write everything, for fear that if I should
escape I might be captured with the book upon me.

"*Jan. 6, 1865.* The 'rebs' took out the new squads
yesterday afternoon, and three of the prisoners ran
away. They do not take any out to-day on account of
the rain, they say. I have a kind of presentiment that
a change, for better or for worse, is about to take place
in my fortunes. Am afraid it is for the worse. Misfor-
tunes never come singly, they say, and they seem to
have begun coming to me when I lost my job outside.

"*Jan. 7, 1865.* No better prospects as yet for the
future, though there is considerable talk of 'general
exchange.' Have been thinking of trying to get out of
this infernal hole. If I could get out on parole to work,
could stay more contentedly, but I can't stand the
pressure here. George has been sick, and is now a
patient in the hospital.

"*Jan. 8, 1865.* Ten months a prisoner. Am going
to try to get out the first dark night.

"*Jan. 9, 1865.* Nothing particular transpired to-
day. Tried to get the lieutenant to let me out on
parole again, but he would not, and so I picked out a
place to climb over the stockade."

The truth is that while I was out on parole I had
studied out a plan for escape, and had been busy working on it from the day my parole ceased. I had noticed

that some of the paroled men who worked in the hospital, and about the commissary department of the
prison, helping to carry in and issue the rations, and to
do other work that required them to pass out and in
frequently, were provided with passes. I had noticed
these passes, and believed I could make one that would
let me pass an ordinary guard, especially after dark.
These passes were written in ink, on the face, in a hand
easily imitated, and were stamped on the back with a
red ink stamp.

My plan was to imitate the handwriting on the
front and make a stamp on the back with a red pencil.
The first thing to do was to get the pencil. I thought
that among 15,000 Yankee prisoners I could either find
one or get it made. So I began to inquire for one.
Soon found that it would be hard to find, so I began
systematically to inquire, going through the whole of
1,000, or detachment, before trying the next. On the
second day I found a man who had a short red pencil,
and secured it. Then I had to get some one who had
a pass, to lend it to me so that I could learn to imitate
it. My recollection is that I got my friend Wardell to
get a pass for me· Do not remember whether I told
him what I wanted to do or not. Anyway I had one of
the genuine passes and set about learning to counterfeit. I began first on the stamp and have now in my
note book, from which these memoranda are copied,
my first effort to make the stamp. It is in this form but
in red:

CHEATHAM

Cheatham was the name of one of the rebel officers. While I sat in my shebang, as we called it, at
work on this stamp, it occurred to me that some man
among those who had such passes might be induced to
let me use a pass to get out with, and then send it in
by some other man.

I knew of no man who had such a pass who would
be likely to trust a stranger with it. No one with whom
I was on terms of intimacy had one, and to ask a
stranger to do for me what might cost him his life,
seemed to be useless. I had nothing to offer as a bribe,
except a few dollars in confed., as we called the rebel
money. My only friend in the camp who had money
was Wardell. The moment I thought of him in that
connection, I knew that the problem was solved. Dick
Wardell we called him,—I suppose Richard was his
name, was then a handsome young man, below medium
height, but well built and in every way a clean-cut,
shrewd Yankee, probably twenty-five years old. He
was one of the chopping squad when we were first
taken out, but he soon obtained what he thought a
better thing.

One of the rebel officers took a fancy to Dick and
hired him to stay in the stockade and exchange confederate money for greenbacks. At that time a dollar of
our money was worth twenty to thirty dollars of rebel
money, at Charleston. The rebel officers were buying
greenbacks in the stockade and selling them at Charleston. They were paying about ten for one. To facil-
itate business, they had forbidden the rebel sutler, who
had a store in the prison, taking any greenbacks from

the prisoners in payment for his goods. The Yankees who had greenbacks must first exchange for confed. before they could trade with the sutler.

I called on Dick Wardell. "Dick," said I, "would you like to get away?"

"You bet your bottom dollar," said Dick.

"Haven't you got a roll of confed. that belongs to a reb?"

"Yes."

"How much?"

"About fifteen hundred."

"Would you be willing to buy your way out with it?"

Dick was an honest fellow and he didn't at first take kindly to the scheme. We talked about it a long time. I told him about my first attempt, how we would be helped by the negroes, and showed him on an old map that Sherman was heading toward Savannah, where we could meet his army without having to go far. We did not then know that Sherman had already taken Savannah. In fact, I persuaded Wardell that as all was fair in love and war, if he could get away by using the rebel's money, he ought to do it. Once in the notion he took hold with a will. He knew a Yankee sergeant who was working in the hospital. The hospital was about an acre of ground in one corner of the stockade, and partitioned off from the remainder of the prison by posts with a rail on top. This sergeant and his squad of about ten men, were all on parole. They were employed building sheds in the hospital (so called) for the sick to lie under. These sheds were made by putting forked logs in the ground, poles on the forks, one being a ridge pole, and the others lower, so as to form a roof when covered with shakes or long shingles. Other men were employed to cut the forks and poles and make the shakes in the woods The sergeant and his men carried them from the woods into the hospital corner of the stockade and put up the sheds.

In order that these men might pass out and in at the hospital gate, they were provided with passes. This sergeant agreed to pass Wardell and myself out for twelve hundred dollars in confederate money. Early on the next morning after this agreement was made, Wardell and I, in order to get into the hospital, procured a stretcher and found a sick man to carry in. Having gained admission to the hospital we found that the sergeant had taken one of his men into his confidence and that we were to use that man's pass.

This plan of escape may, to the reader, seem quite tame, requiring neither nerve nor daring for its execution. To step into line with eight or ten other men, receive a pass, and then walk out of the gate, passing a guard who would merely look at your pass, did seem a simple and an easy thing to do. It was neither simple nor tame nor easy. That guard had a loaded gun. His instructions were to shoot, without halting, any prisoner he saw attempting to escape. We were told that a furlough was granted as a reward to every guard who killed a prisoner attempting to escape. We did not know how many times the guard on duty that morning had been there before. If he had been there before, he might notice a change of one man in the

number entitled to pass.   Should he detect us in our
scheme, he might carry out instructions and shoot us
then and there.   If he did not shoot, but merely handed
us over to the officer on duty, hanging by the thumbs
and thirty days in the dungeon on scant bread and
water, would surely follow.   Few men endured these
tortures who were not by them so broken down in
health and spirit that they soon after succumbed to the
ordinary hardships of the prison life.

It was a dangerous plan, too, for the sergeant.   It
was a violation of the parole under which he was en-
trusted with the passes.   Death was supposed to be the
punishment for violating a parole.   We thought of and
talked of all these things that morning, the sergeant,
Wardell and myself.   More than twenty years have
passed and the vividness with which I recall the incidents of that morning, is evidence to me that one at
least of the three had need to summon up his courage.

The sense of personal danger that one feels under
such circumstances, is not the sole cause of agitated
feeling.   No ambitious student, however carefully
trained, can take the rostrum on his graduating day,
without more or less of fear and trembling.   Many a
lawyer, even after long practice, tries in vain to sleep
the night before an important trial.   They are not of
common mould who can perform a tragical act on the
stage of life without perturbance of soul.   The little
boy giving his name on that first day at school, the
maiden approaching the altar on her bridal day, the
soldier standing in line of battle with the enemy in full
view, it comes alike to all.

Aside from the danger involved, this was to me a critical moment. For ten months, my thoughts by day, my dreams by night, had been of escape. I was about to try. Succeed, and home and mother, father, brothers and sisters, and all that life gives promise of to a boy of nineteen, were before me; fail, and tortures and hunger were sure, and perhaps starvation, sickness, and death.

The sergeant was very anxious to have Wardell go first, because Wardell had the money which he was to hand over when he was on the outside. Wardell insisted on my going first, because I had escaped once, and he thought that I could make a second attempt with greater coolness than one who had never tried, so I stepped into the line and took the pass.

There were nurses and patients of the hospital and workmen all around us, who knew nothing of what was going on. The rest of the men with passes did not know. It seemed to me that every man around me must see in my face all that was in my mind. The guard, to my immense relief, took no more notice of me than of the others. As had been arranged between us, I went to work carrying in poles and shingles with the others. After we had gone out and come in two or three times, the guard concluded that he knew us and ceased to look at the passes. Then the sergeant went out with me, and I gave him back the pass which he was to take in and give to Wardell, while I was to remain out until Wardell should join me. It would not do, however, for Wardell to attempt to pass the same guard. He must wait until that guard's two hours were

up and another took his place. I sat under a tree
waiting; saw the relief guard go round, was expecting
every moment to see Wardell come through the gate,
when I saw the sergeant coming out. I knew in a moment that something had gone wrong. His agitation
was to me evident, from the manner of his walk.
When he got to me he was so badly scared he could
hardly speak. "You must come back in," he said.
"Here, take the pass, go get a load of shakes and come
right in." I asked him what the trouble was. He said
that we were found out; that an officer had come into
the hospital after Wardell just as Wardell was about to
come out.

What had transpired I do not know. I have never
since seen or heard from either that sergeant or Wardell. It occurred to me, however, that the officer for
whom Wardell was exchanging money, had gone into
the stockade to see Wardell on business and had been
told that Wardell had taken a sick man to the hospital,
and that the officer had very naturally gone there to
find him. Anyway, I said to the sergeant that I needed
no pass to come back in. The guard never asked for a
pass from a man who wanted to go in. I told him to go
in and I would go to the woods after the load of shakes
and we would try again some other day. He went in
and I went to the woods, not to get shakes, but to shake
from my feet the dust, from my life, the horrors of that
prison pen.

CHAPTER XXIII.

"*Jan. 10, 1865.* I am a free man to-day, but don't
know how long I shall have the good fortune to remain
so. Last night was a dark night and I had no trouble
in climbing over the stockade. It is noon now and has
commenced to rain."

Such is the entry made in my pocket diary on the
day that I went to the woods for my last load of shakes.
So written for the purpose of misleading my captors,
should I have been recaptured. When I left the sergeant, as before narrated, I walked leisurely toward the
woods, meeting many of the paroled men and some of
the rebel soldiers. No one said anything indicating
suspicion. Some of the rebel soldiers knew me as the
captain of the chopping squad, and probably supposed
I was still out in that capacity. Once in the woods I
avoided meeting anyone and walked rapidly toward the
north. When I had gone what I thought to be about a
mile, I went into the swamp, got into the creek that
flowed through it, and waded up the stream what I
judged to be another mile. By this means I hoped to
avoid leaving any scent for the pack of blood hounds
that were taken every evening around the prison about
two miles out. These hounds were so trained that they
would take and follow the track of any prisoner who

during the day had crossed the limits of the parole. As I waded along in the water thinking I was far enough out to be safe, and feeling pretty tired, for wading up stream in water, and cold water at that, is hard work, it began to rain. Knowing that a hard rain would as effectually remove all scent from my tracks as a running stream, I left the water. I sat down with my back against a large tree, to rest. To keep off the rain, I had secured a large piece of bark and leaned it against the tree and sat under it. Sitting there, protected from the fast falling rain, I wrote the notes last quoted. Had just finished when I heard behind me, voices of men, barking of dogs and the sound of horses' feet. Looking carefully, I saw through the thick woods the squad of rebel cavalry and the pack of blood hounds, passing along a road that crossed the creek in sight of where I sat. Had I kept on wading up the creek I would surely have been so close to them at the crossing, as to have made my discovery by the dogs almost certain. They crossed the creek and stopped at a farm house that stood on a hill, a quarter of a mile or so beyond, and I crossed the dangerous line behind the dreaded hounds, and went rejoicing on my way, the greatest danger to the escaping prisoner from a rebel prison, safely passed. The rain came down in torrents, relieving me from all anxiety in regard to the dreaded hounds. I traveled as nearly as I could tell, North and West, intending to strike the railroad that runs West from Florence, so as to have some guide to go by in the night. Soon after dark I came to a plantation where there were negro quarters, and after some reconnoitering, I entered one,

BLOOD-HOUNDS IN SIGHT.

made myself known, and was received with generous hospitality. A guard was immediately placed so that no man, woman or child of my race might come upon me unawares, and I was warmed and fed in truly chivalrous style by the grateful negroes. Grateful then, for blessings only hoped for, and fearful lest their deeds of gratitude might be discovered, and bring them present woe.

Having rested, and had my clothing well dried, and my shoes dried and softened with grease, I resumed my way along the railroad track. Came into Lynchburg about daylight, and there saw an old " uncle " getting ready to kill hogs. He was building up a great log-heap of dry logs, with " fat " pine for kindling, and putting stones among the logs, with which to heat the water, to scald the hogs, just as I had helped to do often at home. He no sooner learned that I was an escaped Yankee, than he urged me to "get away from hyer, young massa. Too many folks gwine to be around hyer soon." But he told me how to find another black man, whom I could trust, and to him I went. He took me to a safe place in the woods, built for me a nice fire beside a big log; then brought me food and quilts to wrap up in; cared for me as tenderly as a mother does for her sick boy, and then left me there to sleep. My diary reads:

" *Jan. 11, 1865.* It rained until sundown. I was completely soaked. Stopped about 10 o'clock and got my clothes partially dried, then came four miles this side of Lynchburg. It was daylight when I stopped, completely fagged out; was so tired that I could not

have walked another mile. My feet are blistered, and
I am stiff and sore all over. Made a fire in the woods,
and have stayed by it all day. Shall try to reach Sumpterville, twenty-two miles, to-night."

I dared not mention, in my notes, the stranger
friend who built the fire, and bathed my feet, and rubbed my swollen joints, and brought me food and bed,
lest some mishap might cause his left hand to know
what his right hand had been doing.

That night I followed the wagon-road to Sumpterville. Nearing the town, and daylight coming on, I
began to look for some negro quarter, where I could
make myself known, and secure the usual assistance.
At length, I saw near the road two rows of negro quarters. I went among them searching for one, the inmates of which were up. There was a stillness about
them that made me feel suspicious. Negroes are early
risers, and you seldom find them all asleep on any large
plantation. At length, finding no signs of anyone being
awake, I rapped on the door of one of the houses.
After repeated rapping some one called out: " Who's
there?" It was no negro's voice. " Who's there?" came
again, and evidently the voice of a white woman. I
thought best to answer, so I said: " I am a soldier, and
have lost my way." Then I heard: "John, John, wake
up, there is some one at the door." When John awoke
that woman must have had a hard time making him
believe that there had been anybody at the door. I was
wretchedly tired and my feet were painfully sore, but
the first few minutes after leaving that door, I in some
way got over a good deal of ground. I afterward

learned that those negro quarters were occupied by the families of poor white soldiers, who were being cared for by the town, and that some of the soldiers were at home on furlough.

Fearing pursuit, I left the highway and ran off across the fields. As daylight was coming on, it was necessary for me to find a hiding place for the day, so I made for the first plantation in sight—a large one. There I found the usual negro quarters on each side of the street, leading from the planter's house to the fields. Partly to get as far from white people as possible, and partly because there was smoke coming from the chimney, I knocked on the door of a house at the far end of the row. The door was opened by a gentleman of color, but not very much color; probably an octoroon, but as white as myself. Entering, there sat another gentleman of very pale color, dressed in broadcloth, a ring on his finger, a gold watch and chain—a regular dandy—smoking a finely flavored cigar by the fireplace. Well, I thought to myself, as I accepted a proffered cigar and took a seat, this is a pretty kettle of fish; I am in a scrape now, sure. In order to find out how the land lay I kept the two men talking. They were brothers. One was the overseer of the plantation, the other a clerk in a store at Charleston, out on a visit. They were slaves. Gathering from their conversation that their sympathies were on the right side, I made myself and my wants known, and was at once carried off to a safe hiding place in the woods. To build a fire they thought might lead to discovery, so they furnished me with blankets to wrap myself up in while I slept. These men thought the best way for me to get beyond Sumpterville was to go straight through. They said: "Let one of our black boys walk behind you, just as though he was following his master, and no one will suspect you of being a Yankee." There were two battalions of rebel soldiers camped near the town, and they were roaming around everywhere. As I was as likely to meet them one place as another, I took the overseer's advice, and that night I started out, followed by my guide. No negro driver ever appeared less afraid of being noticed than I did, as I stalked through Sumpterville that evening, closely followed by my black slave. I had so little fear of detection that I walked up to the camp-fire of some of the soldiers, smoked a pipe of tobacco, and talked with them some time, taking care, however, to keep some of them talking all the time, and leave as soon as I had got all the information I wanted. These soldiers were on their way to the front to stop Sherman, their train being delayed by the washing away of a bridge. My guide took me a few miles beyond the town and left me with another negro, with whom I stayed the rest of the night and the next day, in order to get my blistered feet in better condition.

CHAPTER XXIV.

"*Jan. 14, 1865.* Did not reach the Santee river last night; it was farther than I thought. I had several narrow escapes, met ten or twelve soldiers at one time; believe they were deserters from Charleston. Met an officer in the road about one o'clock; came upon him unexpectedly and was somewhat confused, but managed to answer his questions, though he did not seem to be very well satisfied with my answers. His name was Captain Beetsom."

Was walking along a well-traveled road, plantation fields each side, and a full moon shining very brightly, when I met the officer mentioned. I heard what I supposed to be two negroes talking in a fence corner, and not being afraid of negroes, did not seek to avoid them. Coming to where they stood talking in the corner of a rail fence, one proved to be a rebel officer.

I said, " How d'y do;" and would have passed along, but the officer indicated an almost commanding desire for further conversation, and I had either to stop or to run.

He wanted to know where I was going, why I traveled so late, where I belonged, etc. I told him I belonged to Major ———'s battalion, giving the name of one of the majors whose command was at Sumpterville, that we were on the way to Branchville when our train was delayed by the bridge being washed away; that my father lived across the Santee; that I had obtained leave to visit my home, and meet the regiment at Branchville.

"What is your father's name?" I gave it. "Where does he live?" "Ten miles beyond the ferry." "In what parish?" That was a stunner. I didn't know what he meant by parish nor the name of any. Unconsciously I began to stammer. He instantly, and probably as unconsciously, sought to assist my impediment of speech by speaking the names of two. Thus assisted, I easily gave one of the names.

His suspicions seemed to be allayed, and we fell into pleasant conversation. Talked of the war and its prospects, of Sherman and his probable movements. He told me of his experience in the Atlanta campaign. How he had been wounded and was now at home on sick leave. Even removed his clothes and showed me where the ball went in, just above his pants' pocket, and where it came out.

When I proposed to go, he very cordially asked me to spend the rest of the night at his house. Couldn't possibly do so; must get to my father's early in the morning and to Branchville the next night. "But you can't cross the river before the ferry goes," he said, "and I will take you there on horseback as soon as we have breakfast and in plenty of time for the ferry. It only makes one trip a day." Thus he pressed me to stay in the kindest and most hospitable manner. I dared not risk it, and still I had no good excuse to offer,

I was in a dilemma, but I cut it short by thanking him for his courtesy and walking off.

Out of sight, my walk became a run, which I kept up for several miles, then stopped to listen. With my ear to the ground I heard the patter of a horse's feet; got behind a tree, and soon after along came the genial officer on his horse, a large revolver in one hand. He passed by and I followed him. Although he rode at a brisk canter, I kept close enough to hear his horse, believing it safer to do so than to run the risk of being ambushed.

A few miles further on he came to a plantation, rode up to the house and aroused the planter. I slipped up close enough to hear all that was said. He had come to the conclusion that I was a deserter. The two men woke up the negroes at the one negro house and searched the house. My pursuer then concluded that he had passed me on the road and went back. The planter went into his house and I was soon in the hands of my friends in the negro quarters. One of these took me to where the ferry crossed the Santee.

The streams at that time were all swollen by the heavy winter rains. The swamp that bordered the Santee on that side was full of water so that the ferry had to make a trip of three miles. I was concealed near the ferry landing, and some negroes who were going across understood my situation and were to make it all right with the ferryman, who was a negro. The ferry came over about ten in the morning, bringing a rebel officer on horseback, who had pistols in the holsters of his saddle. I kept out of his sight until he rode away, then came from my hiding place. When the ferry was about to start, another white man arrived on horseback who wanted to cross also. This man was a surgeon in the rebel army.

The ferry started, the old ferryman poling the boat along in water three or four feet deep, following the opening among the trees made by the submerged wagon-road. We had not gone far before the rebel began to ask me questions. I told him about the same story that I had told the officer in the road the night before. The ferryman, and the other negroes who were crossing and who were helping to push the boat, heard what the rebel was saying, and were evidently alarmed.

There was a canoe or dug-out tied to the side of the boat. The old ferryman spoke to me, saying: "Say da', young massa, can you paddle a canoe?" "I reckon I can," said I. "Then I'se mighty glad if you'd git into dat ar' canoe an' keep it from gittin' smashed up 'twixt de boat an' de trees."

I got into the canoe, well knowing that the darky had planned to get me away from the rebel. I paddled ahead, gradually drawing away from the ferry until a turn in the road put me out of sight, then I paddled with all my might. Reaching the swollen and swift-flowing river, I did not feel safe in the easily tipped canoe. Money wouldn't have hired me to attempt a crossing in such a craft. It was getting dark too. There seemed no other way to do, so I ventured into the rushing water and safely landed on the other side.

Fearing the rebel had regarded me with suspicion,

"SAY, YOUNG MASSA, CAN YOU PADDLE A CANOE?"

and desiring to mislead him, I pulled the canoe out of the water some distance below the road, and hid it in the brush, then concealed myself near enough to the landing to hear what might be said when the boat arrived. The way that old negro lashed me with his tongue when he got over and saw no boat, was amusing. The rebel, too, had thought all the time that I was a deserter. When he rode off, I came out as the smart old darky had expected me to do, and he explained with great gusto how he had done "all dat cussin' jus' to t'row dat white ossifer off from de scent; knowed all de time dat you would turn up roun' hyer sumwheres, soon as dat odder white man done gone out e'n de way."

It will be noticed that in my notes taken as I traveled, little reference is made to the assistance received from colored friends. They furnished me with food, concealed me in some place where I could sleep during the day, either in secluded woods by a fire, or covered up in a fodder or gin house. To have mentioned these things, would have exposed them to possible discovery and punishment. My notes of that crossing are as follows:

"*Jan. 15, 1865.* Did not travel last night. Heard that the swamp was up so that I could not get to the river on foot. Came to the river to-day and had to wade through water up to my shoulders to get there. Some negroes are here who have been waiting two days to get across. They say the ferry is three miles long, and that the boat will not be over until to-morrow.

"*Jan. 16, 1865.* The boat came over to-day. A rebel officer came over with it; managed to escape his notice. Just as we were about to start, a white man, a surgeon in the rebel army, rode up. Did not see him in time to get out of the way, and had to cross over with him. He asked me some troublesome questions, but did not make much."

Having obtained directions from the negroes, I started on toward Branchville.

I walked rapidly until about one o'clock, when, being tired and hungry, and seeing a light in a negro quarter that I was passing, I concluded to rest and get something to eat.

In answer to my rap on the door, "Who's da?" came in a woman's voice. "Is that you aunty?" I said. "Where is uncle? I want to see him." "Who's you prowlin' around dis time o' night?" I told her that I was a white man and had lost my way. She said her man had gone to a "white folks'" house, and that I could go over there to see him. I gave her to understand that I did not want to be seen by any white man, and, if I had told her why, it would have been all right. I prevailed on her to open the door so that I might sit by the fire until uncle got back. I sat down by the fire when she remarked, "Dat fire's gittin' mighty low," and went out. I heard her chopping with an axe and supposed she would be in presently to replenish the fire.

The next thing I heard was, "Come out of that niggah quarter! you damn white —— of a ——." I opened the door and there in the moonlight, twenty yards away, stood a young man in rebel uniform, with a double-barreled shot-gun in his hands.

As I stood in the door-way he gave vent to a perfect volume of oaths and vile epithets, such as, " Come out of that ar' niggah house, or I will blow your d——d head off!" Putting on more assurance than I felt, I said, " You had better find out who you are talking to, sir, before you use such language. If you are so keen to shoot, you better go to the front and try it on the Yanks."

Somewhat cooled down, he then asked me to give an account of myself. I gave him the Sumpterville delayed-train story.

" What regiment does your battalion belong to?" he said. This was another stunner. I did not remember to have heard the number of the regiment. Answering at random, " The 37th South Carolina," I said. " The h—l you do! There ain't no 37th South Carolina. Can't play that game on me. I arrest you, sir."

I stuck to my story, and intimated that a South Carolina soldier must be lamentably ignorant of what was going on in the state if he didn't know that there was a 37th South Carolina. I told him that if he even had this year's almanac in the house, I could prove it to him. He took me into the house, saying that he was going to Orangeburg after breakfast, and that he would take me along and let me convince the provost marshal that there was a 37th South Carolina.

We sat down by the fire. I looked the young man over and concluded that if he undertook to take me to Branchville, as he proposed, in a one-horse buggy and guard me with a shot-gun, there would be trouble on the way. Still the best plan for me was to get out of the scrape by strategy if possible.

The young man belonged to the rebel cavalry. He was at home on a furlough, and was going to Orange-ville that day to get married. His brother had left about one o'clock, so as to reach a station in time for an early train that would take him back to his regiment at Richmond. The negro man had gone with this brother. The negro woman took me for one of the rebel deserters that infested the neighborhood, often robbing chicken-roosts and pig-pens, and making them-selves a terror to the negroes generally. She had chop-ped with the axe to make believe, then ran to the white folks' house, where the people were up to "speed the parting guest," and told them that there was one of the deserters in her house.

The soldier was right about there being no South Carolina regiment numbered thirty-seven. There were more than thirty-seven regiments in the army from South Carolina, but as each city was ambitious to put the first regiment in the field, there was a 1st South Carolina regiment from Charleston, a 1st from Colum-bia, and so on. A 2d, from several places, and so with each number. So, at least, this soldier said. Still, I persistently stuck to my story; claimed that my regi-ment was organized in the northeast corner of the state, was made up lately of home-guards, old men and boys, and I believe he finally concluded that it was poss-ible for him to be wrong.

We sat there talking until nearly breakfast time.

Then the young soldier, taking his shot-gun, went out on the porch, and as he stood there giving some directions about the horse he was to drive to Orangeburg, his sister-in-law came into the room.

She was the wife of the soldier who had left at one o'clock, and mother of a bright little girl of five or six years, whom I held on my knee and had been telling stories to about the Yankees.

The lady expressed the hope that I would have no trouble in making everything right when I got to Orangeburg. Said she was sorry to have her brother-in-law take a prisoner with him when he was going to meet his bride.

Taking my cue from her sympathetic mood, I begged her to intercede for me with her brother-in-law. I told her I only had verbal permission from my officers to leave the command. That the provost marshal would not believe my story; that he would hold me under arrest. That my officers would be sent on from Branchville to the front, and there would be no telling how long I would be held as a prisoner in a guard-house. That my people, my mother and sisters, would be sure to hear of it, and they would be sorely distressed. That I would much rather the news went home that I was shot than that I had been arrested as a deserter. I assured her, with tears in my eyes, on the word and honor of a gentleman, that there was nothing I so much desired as to get to the front where I could fight for my country.

This last was truth; but oh, the lies I told that lady. Was I excusable under the circumstances? Ask some

moral philosopher.   Let him reason it out.   To me,
life was sweet, liberty dear.   If conscience is any guide,
mine at that moment held me guiltless of all wrong.
A man may talk about conscience while he steals your
spoons, but I doubt if such honest tears as mine were
can be made to trickle down his cheeks while he is
doing that which conscience holds to be wrong.

Tears came to the lady's eyes, too.   She went out on
the porch.   I heard, but cannot recall exactly her words.
As I stood there listening, it occurred to me that here
was a sample of that Southern chivalry which I had always believed in, but seldom had a glimpse of.   He
tried to refuse.   She would not let him.

"Why, John," she said, "you must let him go.
Think of his mother and sisters.   What would your
mother and your sisters say?   Think of your Maggie,
John, and this is your wedding day.   Would you have
this boy curse you on your wedding day?   Oh, you
must let him go."   Then her arms went around his
neck, there was one long, resounding kiss, and she
brought in the gun.

The soldier followed her, laughing.   He said he
supposed he would have to let me off, as there was no
use trying to refuse a woman.   We all sat down to
breakfast.   That over, the soldier invited me to ride
with him to where the Branchville road turned off from
that to Orangeville, which I did.   There was no hypoc-
risy in the thanks I tried to express to the lady of that
Southern home, as I took her hand at parting.

At the forks of the road I parted with the young
soldier, wishing him joy at his wedding, and thanking

him warmly for his kindness. "Don't think you have much cause for thanking me," he said, meaning that to his sister-in-law I owed my release. "Well, you have both given me more cause for thanks than you are aware of," I said, turning from him to conceal the smile I could not suppress.

No boy just out of school, no bird just freed from a cage, ever whistled or sung with a gayer heart than mine, as I went merrily on my way that bright frosty morning.

For a while the road led me to a timbered country, but at length I came to where the road was a lane, with cultivated fields on each side. Some distance ahead I saw plantation houses, and concluded to get by them by walking through the corn field on the opposite side.

Nearing these houses I saw a white man on the porch, and perceived at the same time that he was watching me. Presently he shouted and motioned to me to come to him. I kept on, as though I had neither seen or heard. Then he called to some one to loose the dogs, and gun in hand, started on the run in my direction.

Naturally fleet of foot and long-winded, I was soon in the woods, beyond that corn field, and glad to find a swamp there. Wet ground at first, then a little water, then ankle deep. Straight on I ran, knowing that no ordinary white man could keep me in sight, and that dogs could not track me through water. When I had gone far enough to feel perfectly safe, I climbed into some wild vines, where I could rest and be out of the water, and there I stayed until dark.

That was a hard night. It rained and was pitch dark. I could not see the trees; had to feel for them with a stick. I fell over logs, got tangled in vines, pricked by thorns and scratched by briars.

Toward morning, guided by the sound of crowing cocks, I got out of the swamp, and found a negro quarter. Woefully tired, famished for food, wet to the skin, with torn and muddy clothes, and bleeding wounds, I was surely a pitiable object as I stood by the pitch pine fire those trusty darkies built for me.

CHAPTER XXV.

I STEAL MULES AND TAKE A RIDE—A WELL-LAID SCHEME "GANG AFT AGLEE"—SOME DANGEROUS PLACES—CROSSING THE SALKAHATCHIE.

That day, January 17, I was furnished with some ~~some~~ dry clothes, was well warmed and fed, and laid away in a fodder house while my shoes and pants were repaired. Was considerably disgusted to learn that I was only three miles from the place where the man took after me in the corn field. I had spent the night traveling, in more or less of a circle, in the swamp that bordered Cattle Creek. Was now twelve miles southeast of Branchville. Desired to cross the Edisto River. Heavy rains had swollen all the streams and filled the swamps with water. All the streams in that part of South Carolina run from northwest to southeast. As I was making for Savannah, my route lay across all the streams and swamps. Nearly all of the roads run parallel with the streams. The inhabitants of the country were in a state of excitement and alarm, apprehending an invasion of the state by Sherman's army. Rebel soldiers were being collected at Branchville and other points, and preparations made to meet the invader. The masters feared that their negroes would rise en masse, and go to meet their deliverers. Desertion from the rebel troops were frequent. The ferries and bridges on all important streams were guarded, and mounted patrols were upon all the highways. Under these circumstances it was exceedingly difficult for me to pass through the country. Even the negroes, always so willing to furnish food, or to travel at night as guides, were afraid to stir out by night, lest they be caught by the patrols, and killed for example. I spent two days and nights trying to find some unguarded place where I could cross the Edisto.

Finally, I met a young negro, who told me there was no guard on the bridges that crossed the two Edisto Rivers above where they came together. He said the water was so deep between the two bridges that no guard was necessary. This boy had daring enough for anything. He wanted to take me across these bridges, which he said he could reach by wading and swimming, but as it was ten miles from his home to the nearest bridge, he was afraid he could not make the trip and get back in one night.

I suggested that we borrow a couple of his master's mules and ride. He was willing to run the risk of being caught putting the mules into the stable when he should return, but was not willing to risk being caught trying to take them out. So about 11 o'clock that night, while the negro boy was conveniently posted so as to give a signal in case of danger, I slippped into the barn and brought out a span of mules.

We had to ride bareback, because the saddles were at the house, where they could not be easily obtained. I had wondered how this boy expected to pass the patrol on the road, traveling this way. Usually when I traveled with a negro for guide he walked ahead, and there was little danger of our meeting any white man

whom his quick eye or attentive ear did not first discover. I asked this boy how we were to get by the patrol on mules. "Don' you gib yourself no troubble
'bout dat, young massa; ain't gwine to meet no patrol
on dat road what I'se gwine to trabble. You stick to
dat ar mule, and I'se gwine to land you safe on todder
side o' bofe dem ar Edisto Ribbers." I did stick to the
mule, and there was little danger of meeting patrols on
the road he "trabbled."

It was through fields, over fences, and through by-
paths in the woods. How he could tell where he was
going in the dark puzzled me. We were several times
in water that caused the mules to swim before we
reached the first bridge, and had to swim in several
places between the bridges, but he landed me safe
across both Edistos, and did not leave me until he had
turned me over to another negro two miles beyond.

Riding bare-back on a mule was to me a new kind
of exercise. The parts that rested on the mule were so
badly excoriated, that for several days I could not walk
in a natural manner.

The next night I passed through Midway, and stopped with a negro who was a coachman for his master,
and was going to cross the Salkahatchie to bring his
master home. This river was also guarded. Troops
under the rebel Hardee, and the cavalry general,
Wheeler, were making preparations to meet and op-
pose Sherman, should he attempt to come that way.
The greatest uncertainty prevailed as to what route
Sherman would take. The course that seemed to be
best for me, was to go toward Savannah as rapidly as

possible, provided I could get through the lines of the enemy.

I anticipated difficulty in getting over the Salkahatchie, for along that stream the rebels were preparing to make a stand. Not only bridges and causeways were guarded, but there was also a line of pickets close enough to be in sight of each other, walking their beats all along the stream. When the negro proposed to take me in a close carriage through this army of rebels and across a guarded bridge and causeway, I thought it a good scheme. He had a pass which read: "Pass my black boy, Sam, and carriage," and was signed by a colonel. We had arranged that in case the carriage should be stopped and questions asked, I was to claim to be a relative of the colonel on a visit to the family. If the guard at the bridge refused to let me over, I was to get out and pretend to be waiting for the return of the carriage, until I could secede. But "the best laid schemes of mice and men gang aft aglee." After waiting all one day and night for this chance to ride in a colonel's coach, it turned out in the morning when we were ready to start that one of the ladies of the family had concluded to ride over after the colonel. Had I been better clad and sufficiently posted as to what regiments were camped beyond the river, it would have been fine work, and feasible, to have introduced myself to this family and secured a ride under the protection of the pass. As it was, I had no time for preparation, and thought best to try some other plan.

I remained all that day in the negro quarters where two women were at work carding and spinning wool.

About noon two of Wheeler's cavalry rode up, hitched their horses and came into the house and ordered the women to get dinner for them. I had crawled under a bed when these men approached the house. One of them said he had been up all night and would take a nap while the dinner was cooking, so he came into the room where I was and lay down on the bed that I was under. I did not sleep while I was there.

As soon as it was dark I resumed my journey, keeping the traveled road that led to the river; met a good many people, and some on horseback overtook and passed me. None of them saw me, however.

My sense of hearing had become so acute that I could hear even the footsteps of a man long before I could distinguish his form by starlight, while the gallop of a horse, I verily believe I could hear, when listening with my ear to the ground, for half a mile. Once, while sleeping in the woods in the daytime, I was awakened by the sound of approaching footsteps, and on looking around, saw a negro at least a hundred yards away, coming with my dinner.

I had resolved that night, having become well rested, to cover a long distance. I had not gone far when I came to where some soldiers had camped by the side of the road. I made a long detour in the woods to get by them, and when I came to a road, supposed it was the same I had been on, and walked until nearly morning before finding out that the soldiers were camped where two roads crossed, and that the one I had taken ran at right angles to the way I wanted to go. Toward morning I found a large number of ne-

groes, men, women and children, sleeping in an
old unused store building at somebody's corners.
They had been brought from a plantation near
Savannah to keep them from running away to Sherman. They told me to cross the Salkahatchie and
travel down the west side, and I would come to Sherman's men, sure.

The next night I traveled to within a mile of where
the rebels, under Hardee, were building fortifications
and guarding the bridge and causeway that crossed the
river and the swamp. This was the place the negro
had proposed to take me over in the carriage. I think
he called it Brunson's bridge. After hiding during the
day as usual, I concluded to find some negro who would
go with me as a guide, before attempting to pass the
guards and cross the river.

About 11 o'clock that night I entered the cabin of
an old negro, to whom I had been directed, and sat
talking with him by the fire, when four or five "Johnnies" opened the door without knocking, and came in.
They were from a camp near by. All very young. I
began at once to ask them what regiment they belonged
to, what they were doing out so late, and to the immense delight of the old negro, who was at first badly
scared, I kept them talking, first one and then another,
about soldier life and Sherman, until they were ready
to go, and not one of them thought of asking me where
I belonged.

These men wanted to buy chickens and eggs, and
the old man hastened their departure by telling them
to come right along with him and he would show them

a black man who would take them to a plantation where there were plenty.

On his return the old man said the safest way to cross the river was to go south to where it spread out, and formed what was called Whippey Swamp, and that I had better not try it without having some black man, who knew the swamp well, for a guide. He then went with me several miles, and left me with another negro. This man knew of two negroes, who had been brought from their master's home near Savannah, and who had run away, and were now trying to get back. They were now hiding in the woods, waiting for a night dark enough to enable them to crawl between the guards that were posted all along the edge of the swamp. He proposed to put me under their care.

The next day this man and his wife (they had no children) left me locked up in their cabin, and went to work in some field, so far away that they did not return for dinner. At night the woman came back alone, saying her husband had gone to find out about the runaways.

I had eaten supper, and was enjoying a pipe by the fire, when we were startled by a rapping on the door. The woman had locked it by pulling the latch string to the inside. In other words, the latch string wasn't out. To her question, "Who's da'?" the answer came: "Soldiers, aunty. What you got yor do' fastened fah? Hurry up and let us in." She motioned to me to get into the bedroom, and she made all the noise she could. so that mine might not be heard. When she opened the door the two men came in. Said they must have some washing done, and despite her protests, saying she had worked hard all day, and couldn't possibly do it, they proceeded to take off the shirts and drawers that she must wash while they sat by the fire in pants and coat. They paid no attention whatever to her protests; just told her to go right along and do it, and that she wouldn't get anything for it either, if she made any more fuss about it.

In the back part of the bedroom there was a kind of a window—a square opening in the wall, with a board door hung on leather hinges, and fastened on the inside. I tried to open this and get out, but the door fitted into the frame so that it would not open without noise. The woman probably heard the noise, and understood what I was trying to do, for she came into the bedroom and got a padlock and chain, and proceeded to lock the bedroom door from the outside, putting the chain through a crack in the partition and hole in the door. Under cover of the noise she made I pushed the back window open and crawled out. She soon came out to put her kettle on for the washing, such work usually being done out of doors, and gave a low whistle. This I answered, and she came and told me where to hide until her husband returned.

The two soldiers belonged to some general's body-guard. The general had put up for the night at the white folks' house of the plantation, and the guards had camped in the yard. This the negro learned when he came back, and also where they were from and all about them. When he was ready to start away with me we passed along by their camp, and I lit my pipe at their fire and talked awhile with them. Stated to them that I belonged to one of the regiments that were camped up at the bridge and was out after provision. Partly because it was my mother tongue and partly by practice, I had learned the we'uns and you'ns, the broad a's and the no r's until, as this negro and many others told me, there was no danger of anyone suspecting me of being from the North.

Accompanied by my negro guide, I walked several miles to the cabin of another man who knew where the runaways were concealed. There I had to wait while the runaways were sent for.

As I sat by the big log fire which was burning in the old-fashioned fireplace, talking to a lot of negroes who had gathered there, about the war, the Northern army and the proclamation of Lincoln, that freed every slave, suddenly and without warning, in walked the master.

He was a tall, slender man with gray hair and long gray beard, a typical Southern gentleman. It was so late at night that we had not expected such an interruption, or a guard would have been placed to give warning. I had noticed the black eyes and shining white teeth of several little pickaninnies peeping in at the cracks of the cabin a little while before, but did not apprehend any danger from them. One had gone to the big house and told the massa that there was a white man in the negro house.

Here he was, anger flashing from his eyes and ready to resent, if not to punish, a violation of a rigidly enforced Southern rule. No white man was allowed to enter another negro's quarter without the consent of the master.

Knowing this, I rose instantly, and before the old man had begun to vent his ire, I was making an apology. "You must excuse me, sir," I said, "for being in your negro quarters without your permission. I belong to General ———'s body-guard. We are camped at Mr. ———'s plantation. The large army under Hardee *a* near there, have about used up everything on the place, and I came down here to see if I could find some chickens and eggs for my mess. I thought it was too late to disturb you, and was waiting here while one of your men went to hunt up some provisions for me. I trust, sir (the old man had on a blue Yankee overcoat) that the color of your coat does not indicate your sentiments. If it does, you will have to excuse me from making any apology whatever."

This shot struck home. The old man straightened up and eloqently repelled the insinuation. He related with pride the sacrifices he had made to defend his country against the hired robbers of the black abolition ruler. He had sent his children and his grandchildren. All of his kith and kin able to bear arms were in the confederate armies, where they would spill the last drop of their blood rather than let the feet of the ruthless invader trample the sacred soil of South Carolina. "This coat, sir, was captured in honorable combat, and sent to me as a trophy of the war. As such, I am proud to wear it." It was easy to keep the old gentleman talking. In the meantime, one of the young negroes slipped out to warn those who had gone after the runaways, and might be returning, of the situation. When the old man had talked his talk out, he invited me to go with him into the house and spend the night. Said he had a relative there on a visit who was a young man and a soldier like myself. An officer of Wheeler's cavalry. Thought two soldiers would enjoy visiting together. He pressed the invitation in truly chivalrous fashion. I regretted very much that I was obliged to return as soon as possible to camp, and could not therefore accept. Then he pressed me to just come in and have a glass of peach brandy and a cigar. To get around that I pleaded great haste and promised to come down the next day and call on his relative and swap war stories with him. The planter returned to his house not seemingly well pleased, and I did not linger there to learn the effect his report might have on the visiting officer from Wheeler's cavalry.

I was then taken about two miles and put in charge of the two runaway negroes. They had arranged to cross the swamp that night. Their preparations were all made. They had an axe, some pitch pine torches, and had selected a place where there were weeds and brush, to cross the beat of the rebel guard.

We passed the guard and gained the edge of the swamp. Here our first difficulty was the thin ice that had formed on all of the still water. This was the coldest night I had experienced in that state, and the only one that I remember being cold enough to freeze ice on a stream.

To break this ice without making sufficient noise to alarm the guard, rendered our progress for the first two or three hundred yards exceedingly slow.

When fairly into the swamp, we lit the pine torches. Here we found the undergrowth of brush and vines almost impenetrable. The water was from two to four feet over that part of the swamp that would have been dry ground during the summer season. The streams where the current was we either had to bridge by cutting small trees and falling them across the stream. There was ice to break wherever there was no current. We were soon wet from head to foot, often falling in the matted vines and sometimes stepping into deep holes. One of the negroes was of middle age, the other a mere boy. A hardy man used to exposure can stand an hour or so of that kind of work and call it rather tough, but a whole night's struggle through thorns and briars, on turning logs and slippery poles, sometimes breaking ice, sometimes swimming in ice-cold water, will try the endurance of the toughest man. The boy's courage soon gave out. When we came to a small island where there was dry ground he lay down, and declared, his limbs shaking and his teeth chattering all the while, that " he would radda' die right den and da' dan to go eny fudda'." He would not be persuaded and we could not carry him. The man cut a good, withy switch and warmed his jacket.

It was broad daylight when we got over, so numbed and stiffened with cold that we could scarcely move. We had kept a torch burning, otherwise we could not have built a fire. I thought I never would get warm, and my teeth would never cease to chatter, nor my body to ache. I stayed by that fire all day, striving in

GUIDED THROUGH A SWAMP BY RUNAWAY SLAVES.

vain to get warm. At night a negro, sent by the runaways, took me to his cabin, and doctored me up with
pepper tea and hot victuals, then wrapped in quilts and
hid in a fodder house. I remained that night and the
next day. I did not deem it prudent to keep in company with the runaways, because if captured with them
I would surely be killed, and I could not be seen with
them by any white man without his suspicions being
aroused.

CHAPTER XXVI.

"THE GIRL I LEFT BEHIND ME" — THE GRAND OLD FLAG
AND THE BOYS IN BLUE — I AM DUBBED "SMOKED
YANK."

I was now on the west side of the Salkahatchie,
between thirty and forty miles from Pocotalago, where
a portion of Sherman's army was in camp. There were
no more rivers or swamps in my way and there was a
well traveled road to follow, but there were swarms of
rebel cavalry and rebel citizens all around me, watching
for the approach of Sherman's army, picking up deserters and moving their slaves and other property to more
secure places. There were white men on guard at
every plantation and the negroes were in such a state
of anxiety and terror, and so suspicious of a white man,
that I found it almost impossible to communicate with
them. They seemed afraid to talk with me or help me
in any way, lest I should turn out to be a spy seeking to
betray them.

I was obliged to use the utmost caution and to
travel only by day because I could get no guide, and if
I traveled at night I could not tell where or when I
might run on to the patrols or ambushed guards.
Wearily and stealthily I crept along the edge of the
swamp a mile or so from the road, making only ten or
twelve miles in a day. Often when I could not find
cotton or fodder in which to hide, I had to shiver with
cold all night. The last three or four days were the

most difficult and trying of my journey. I did not get food but two or three times and I hardly slept at all, but the thought of freedom, now so near, nerved me up, and in a measure compensated for lack of food and sleep.

About nine o'clock in the forenoon of February 1st, I began to hear a rumbling sound which I knew must be made by loaded wagons moving on the road. Whether they belonged to retreating rebel or an advancing Union army, I could not tell, and I dared not take the risk of finding out.

About noon, as I was moving cautiously along, peering in all directions from behind one tree before slipping to another, suddenly there burst upon my listening ears the joyous notes of "The Girl I Left Behind Me," played by a full brass band. I knew that there was no rebel army with brass band in that vicinity, and I started on a full run toward the welcome sound.

Reader, I can but faintly describe to you the kaleidscopic pictures which flashed across my mental vision during those supreme moments, as I ran, with hope before and fear behind. Home, father, mother, brother, sisters, the grand old flag, the boys in blue, these for an instant before me, and my feet seemed to spurn the passing ground—then, as the deeds of a lifetime rush together into the memory of a drowning man —there rose up every scene that I had witnessed, or heard described, of the tortures inflicted on escaped prisoners brought back; the tearing of blood-hounds, the hanging by the thumbs, the agonies of the stocks; these behind, and I would turn in mortal terror, almost

hearing the halt! halt! of dreaded pursuers. Thus, with
mingled feelings of joy and fear, I ran on for nearly a
mile through thick woods.   Coming to an opening in
the woods I climbed on to a fallen tree, and there across
a field, marching in the road, with band playing and
colors flying, go the boys in blue.   I take off my hat and
try to shout.   I cannot.   My heart is in my throat.   My
strength is gone.   I recline against the limbs of the tree,
and sob and cry like a child, and wonder whether my
strength will come back, or whether I must sit there
helplessly and let that army go by.

There was a slough in front of me, across that a
house, and a road leading from the house down the side
of the field to the road where the army was marching.
Two men ride up to the house, and as they see me, and
draw their revolvers, my strength returns.   I throw up
my hands and call to them not to shoot, that I am an
escaped prisoner.

These men belonged at the headquarters of Hazen's division of the Fifteenth Army Corps.   One of
them was an orderly, and the other, Pete McDowell,
was quartermaster.   McDowell was from La Crosse,
Wisconsin, where one of the companies of my regiment
was enlisted, and I had no trouble in satisfying him that
I was what I represented myself to be.   They secured
for me a place to ride, and I camped that night with
General Hazen's orderlies.   They were all young men,
about my own age, and they treated me with great
kindness.   They sat up that night until a late hour listening to my account of prison life and of my escape.
One of them, a bright young man, who was General

AND THERE WITH COLORS FLYING AND BAND PLAYING GO THE BOYS IN BLUE.

Hazen's private orderly, and who was nick-named Stammy, because he stammered, declared that I had earned the garter, and insisted on performing the cere- mony of knighthood before I went to bed. He had no- ticed my unavailing efforts to remove with soap and water the effects of pitch-pine smoke from my hands and face, and so, drawing his sword, he delivered an impromptu, humorous harangue, slapped me on the back with the flat of the blade, and dubbed me " *The Smoked Yank.*"

I kept no diary from the 18th of January to the 1st of February, because I lost my pencil and could not get another. The morning after reaching the army I wrote, " February 2."

" The army was in motion early this morning. I had breakfast—never knew before how much I liked coffee—then rode with Stammy, General Hazen's or- derly, up to General Sherman's headquarters. I re- ported to the adjutant-general. The general was standing near, heard me, and took me into his room. He seemed very much concerned about the condition of the prisoners at Florence. He made notes on a map of all that I could tell him about the rebel armies and the places where I had crossed the large streams and swamps. He said that some ambulances would go back to Pocotaligo to-day and that I could go with them and go home, or could go with the army to the sea again, and then go home. I told him I preferred to remain with the army. He called the adjutant and told him to see that I was provided for. The adjutant said he would get me a horse and arms, and that I could join the escort. I prefer to remain with the boys at Hazen's headquarters with whom I am already acquainted."

I rode that day with Stammy in a two-horse carriage which he had captured, and was taking along, as he said, to give the old man (meaning Hazen) a ride once in a while. Stammy was the pet of the division. I still wore my rebel jacket, the same that Barrett took from me, but which I had recovered before leaving Florence. As we rode along every now and then some soldier would call out and say, " Hello there, Stammy! Where did you get that Johnnie?" Stammy would say, " Th-th-is a-a-int n-n-no J-J-Johnnie, th-th-is is a Smo-o-ked Yank." In this way he introduced me all along the line, and *Smoked Yank* was the only name I was known by in that army.

Within a few days I secured a horse, a revolver and carbine, and began to take part in the great march. My regiment was not with Sherman's army, and I was therefore a detachment of myself, commanded only by myself. I got acquainted with Howard's scouts and rode with them whenever they had work to do that I cared to take part in, but whether with them, or with the common " bummers," I was always at the head of one or the other of the columns. The following is a sample from my note book:

" *Feb. 9.* Second Division, 15th Corps, reached the south branch of the Edisto to-day. The bridge had been partly destroyed. Some logs were piled up on the other side forming a kind of breastwork. Myself and three others were on the advance. It looked as though there might be rebs behind the logs. I left my horse and crawled along on the inside of a corn-field fence to find out. About eighty yards from the logs I stopped behind a clump of china trees. As I lay there on the ground watching, I saw a man's head over the logs. I was just drawing a bead on him, when about twenty rebels arose with a yell and fired at me. The balls struck all around me and sent the bark flying from the trees. They called out, "Come in you Yank! Come in you Yank!" There was enough of the bridge left for a man to cross on. I had no notion of coming in. As soon as our boys farther back began to fire, the rebs dodged down, and I got up and ran through the corn-field. They fired on me again, but I was not hit, though it was a close call—shall be more careful hereafter."

The night before the city of Columbia was captured, Hazen's division camped near the river opposite the city. The rebels shelled us during the night. I slept that night near Hazen's tent with my head against the body of a large tree. In the morning, before I had made my toilet, General Logan rode up to see Hazen. As he sat on his horse near my tree, waiting for Hazen to dress and come out, a cannon-ball passed through the top of the tree cutting off some limbs. Hazen came out of his tent, and Logan, who was in a jovial mood, with a gesture toward the city, said: "Hail, Columbia, happy land, if this town ain't burned, then I'll be damned!"

A little while after I saw Logan again. He had a rifled cannon in a road that led to one of the burned bridges. When the gunners had the cannon loaded, Logan would sight it, then climb on to the high bank

beside the road, adjust his field-glass, give the order to
fire, and watch to see where the ball would strike. If
I remember rightly, he was aiming at the State House,
and aiming well, for he would wave his hat and call for
three cheers for South Carolina after each discharge.
He was having a high old time.

When the pontoon bridge was ready, I crossed it
with Howard's scouts and rode into the city. We were
the first into the city, and saw many rebel soldiers, officers and men, taking leave of their friends.

That night the great fire broke out which destroyed
a large portion of that beautiful capital, and left thousands of people houseless and homeless. Many of these
applied for permission to accompany our army when
we continued our march. They were called refugees,
and were divided up among the divisions of the 15th
Corps. General Hazen asked me to take charge of the
refugee train that was assigned to his division. I did
so. Ten infantrymen were detailed as guards and for-
agers and placed under my orders, and I was instructed
to subsist my command from the commissary department of the enemy. I soon had the infantrymen well
mounted on captured mules and horses, and while I had
charge of them, Hazen's refugees did not suffer for
anything that the state of South Carolina could furnish.
There were some old men, but the greater portion of
these refugees were women and children. Among
those in my train were the wife and two charming
daughters of a Lieutenant Thompson, who was one of
the officers at Florence prison at the time I escaped.

At Fayetteville, N. C., General Sherman issued an

order requiring all of the refugees and escaped prisoners to go with an infantry regiment down the Cape
Fear River to Wilmington. I started with the rest,
supposing that I would have charge of my train as before. We traveled until noon and then stopped for dinner. I rode up to the officer who had been placed in
command and made some inquiries. He informed me
that the refugees from that time on must forage for
themselves. I suggested that it would be better to have
a party of infantry mounted, and undertook to tell him
how the refugee trains had previously been managed.
He cut me short, and in a pompous manner ordered me
to go back where I belonged, saying he would send for
me when he needed advice. My recollection is, that
Sherman had sent this officer away from the army because his services were not considered indispensable.
Not caring to serve under such a commander, I rode
back that night and reported to General Hazen the
next morning.

From Fayetteville to Goldsboro, the rebel General
Johnson was in our front and on our left flank, and
there was considerable fighting every day. During the
battle of Bentonsville my desire to see the fighting
led me too far to the front, and I came near being
gobbled up by a squad of rebel cavalry that I ran on to
in some thick woods. Reaching a safe position, concluded to find General Sherman, so as to see how a
great commander would act while a battle was in progress. I found him and his staff in the yard in front of
a farm house. The general was walking back and forth
in the shade of some large trees. When not receiving

messages and sending orders he acted like a very nervous and greatly excited man. He had a cigar in his mouth, and stepping up to an officer who was smoking, asked him for a light. The officer handed him his cigar. As the general lit his own cigar he seemed to be listening to the noise of the battle. Suddenly he turned, dropped the officer's cigar on the ground, and walked off puffing his own. The officer looked at him a moment, then laughed, picked up the cigar and continued his smoke.

When we reached Goldsboro, I learned from General Hazen that Sherman was going to City Point to meet General Grant, and that the army would probably remain some time in camp. I concluded to go home. I had a fine English fox-hunter mare that I had captured on the march. She was the best riding horse I had ever ridden, and very handsome. General Sherman's adjutant-general had noticed and admired my horse, and when I learned that Sherman was about to go to City Point, I told the adjutant-general that if he would arrange so that I could go home from Goldsboro on the first train, that I would make him a present of the fox-hunter. He so arranged, and I left Goldsboro on the train which took Sherman and some of his staff to New Berne. From there I proceeded to Washington, where through the influence of the letters provided for me by the adjutant-general, I secured at the war department without delay, back pay, commutation of rations and clothing for the time I was in prison, and transportation home. A few days after my strange dream came true, except that I met my father first on the hill.